Smell It

Smell It

stories by
Hal Niedzviecki

Coach House Books ⌐ 1998

First edition
ISBN 1-55245-016-3 (bound) ISBN 1-55245-026-0 (pbk.)

With gratitude to:
Ken Sparling, for his editorial acumen, encouragement & friendship.
Hilary Clark, for her editorial judgement, encouragement & friendship.
Sam and Nina Niedzviecki for their constant, unwavering support,
for everything.

Special thanks to Stan Bevington (along with all the Coach House
mad boys), Hoge Day, John Degen and the students and faculty of
the Bard College M.F.A. program.

I am grateful for the kindness and bravery of all the periodicals who
used stories from this collection. The following mags are very fine
reading: *the Quarterly, Ink, the New Quarterly, Prism International,
Black Cat 115, Qwerty, Sub-Terrain, blood + aphorisms, Schrodinger's
Cat, Fish Piss, This Magazine, Queen Street Quarterly, the Writing
Space Journal* and *Taddle Creek*.

Cover art by Hoge Day
Author photo by Mark Lyall

Online at http://www.chbooks.com

CANADIAN CATALOGUING IN PUBLICATION DATA

Niedzviecki, Hal, 1971
Smell It
ISBN 1-55245-016-3 (bound) ISBN 1-55245-026-0 (pbk.)

I. Title.
PS8577.I364S5 1997   C813'.54   C97-932248-0
PR9199.3N54S5 1997

For Jimmy! For Boojdee! For Jimmy!

Wake Up And Find It Gone

She thinks he is having an affair. How can you live in a place, and not have a life in that place? she asks. This is not the only question she asks. There will always be affairs. There will always be the past. He gestures at the spot in front of them. He puts his hand on her leg. This is not the moment she says: I know, I know, am I being crazy? I'm being crazy. Don't tell me I'm being crazy. She turns over and it is not that she is giving up or letting him do it. He aims and she puts it in. Oh, she says. She does not say it to make him feel good. She tells him to do it. She wants him to do it. He does it. Don't I love you? he asks. She stands in front of him. She nods. He wants to stop it right where it is. He wants to touch the ruffle between her breasts. There, he says. How can they be there? One hundred, one hundred and one, one hundred and two. He counts to make it last longer. She is sure that something must matter. Love, she says, is not enough. Enough is enough, he says.

Events Can Be Louder

The voices are a map.

It's your grandfather, she says. He's had a fall.

He puts his head in his hands.

There are two landscapes. The function of one is to limit the other.

He sees objects all around. He can comprehend what surrounds him, while only imagining his presence in those surroundings.

Certain people he knows, even personally, are prepared.

This Local Cinema

He was on his knees when the lightning struck. He was praying, only he wasn't. He was more than hoping though. He was trying to get the door shut. The wind and the rain pulled against him. There was something in the way. Something someone had put there to keep the door open. He was on his knees prying at the rock jammed in there under the crack of the door. C'mon rock c'mon door c'mon door c'mon c'mon. That's when the lightning struck. He watched it hit. He covered his ears with his hands and trapped the sound of it. Sound and light mixed up with that other almost prayer stuff.

He ate a piece of chocolate. When he spit on his dick, his spit was brown.

The window was open. The neighbour's music: *boom boom boom*. The steady beat of rain. He imagined the rain falling on his belly, beating on it.

A breeze danced in the cold drops.

The mosquitoes could not get in when it rained. Otherwise, yes, the mosquitoes would get in. Then he would have to decide: Was it better to be hot or be bitten?

When he finished, he finished big.

What if he walked out of his apartment and down the stairs and out into the street? Why not wash it away, all the brown and stickiness?

She went with him to the place where he was going. They got there. The sun was gone.

He made motions to sit.

He sat.

He spoke in a loud voice:

"If I say to someone who is my friend, someone like John, if I say to John, John, I love Taylor, I am saying that, but really I am saying something else, something I don't know how to say."

She stood where they were. It was dark.

What is interesting is not the way he sees. Not even what he has gone to see.

He closes his eyes. The worst happens.

The camera keels and screeches and the worst happens.

He eats popcorn by the handful, then has to shit so bad he can barely make it home.

He does get home. Arms out to his sides he pushes the night through. The movie is different for him now that he is alone. Almost everything he thinks is leaving him alone.

Lines

He had a hard time recalling.

"C'mon," somebody said.

"Just spit it out," another said.

"Something about a droopy eyelid," he said.

"And?" somebody said.

"So?" another said.

"There's more," he said. His eyes were watching the ceiling. Lines of light, cars passing, lies on the open street. "Something about her condition," he said. "She said: 'they think it can be controlled.' No. Something else. She said: 'It can probably be controlled.'"

The room got dark.

"I've sat next to people like that," somebody said.

"I've felt them crying very near me," another said.

He put his head in his hands. He couldn't see through his hands. The room was getting darker.

The next thing he knew, he was holding on. She was shaking.

Suburb

He puts his fist up and hits the boy. The boy falls with a thunk. The head rolls slowly away from the body. We'll glue it, his father says, squeezing his shoulder. Certainly there are things that can be done. Once a girl came to his room and let him lick the top of her breast. He needs air. He smells old people.

He has taken to borrowing their health problems. A jar of antacid sits on his night-table. He empties five tablets onto his palm. Chalky dust covers the snapshot next to his lamp. He picks the picture up and blows on it. His grandfather smiling at his grandmother. They hated each other. She died neglected. He kept snapping pictures.

And You?

I remember being on the sidewalk, outside the store. It was one of those days. It was so cold the streets were white. He made us wait outside because he didn't have enough money for ice creams. He knew we'd want ice creams so he made us wait outside. We waited outside. He bought us popsicles. I think he spent his last dollar on popsicles. People looked at us, standing outside on the sidewalk sucking popsicles. It was minus fifteen. The wind was blowing. I was happy.

I had this job delivering bundles. Every month, the people were different. I got used to a man and the next month that man was gone. It felt good to get out of the house in the morning.

Sometimes I turn on my computer. Lately, I've been having difficulty clearing my throat. I make a loud noise. It scares people in other rooms.

I'm not worried. I figure it doesn't matter. The hardest thing I ever did was keep from trying.

When Next I've Fallen Home

She calls and he picks up the phone. He wants to say: What, are you crazy, calling me now, with squid ink all over my hands? His hands are wet, slippery. She is crying. It sounds like she is crying.

Dark beetles of ink running down his arms. Her on the phone having an emergency. Not an emergency: A crisis.

Next door someone is learning English.

"Fazze," he hears somebody say. Words through an accented silence. "Eyzzs. Nozzs. Erzzs."

"Stop it," he said. "Can't you stop it?"

He turned back to the computer screen. He started to type. He stopped typing.

"Didn't I ask you to stop it? Didn't I?"

She dropped her arms to her sides, closed her eyes, held her breath.

"Don't do that now," he said. He got up halfway, slumped down. He sighed. He punched the wall.

"I can't work," he said. "Fuck. Fuck."

She opened her eyes, her hands fluttered over her chin, the thin break of nails against her teeth.

"Fine," he said, "Don't stop. I don't care. I don't care what you do."

Just her nails, bitten shells. She took her hands away from her soft lips, her face exposed, her chest pulling against the air. She picked up the book next to her and opened it. She put the book down, spine spread, pages flat against the comforter. Her hands, poised, uncertain. He stopped typing, scowled over at her.

"Don't leave the book like that," he said. "Why do you have to put the book like that?"

She looked up at him.

"Don't cry," he said. "Why are you crying?"

꜁

He wakes up, goes to the bathroom, takes a wet shit.

He comes back to the bed. Early Saturday morning, a thin light through the curtains.

She's asleep, but when he gets up to go to the bathroom she moves, stretching out and stirring a little – a groan, a sigh, the echoed howl of an articulated dream. He looks at her. He looks at the light welling up against the sheet, pressing to get in.

Maybe it's because he loves her so much.

Maybe it's because his asshole still burns.

Maybe it's the terrific fragility of morning, and her, part of it, just lying there, more asleep than he could ever be.

꜁

He was standing there. His basket, empty. The fruit in front of them, pyramids – a cascade of colours, textures. He couldn't seem to step away. They would all come rolling down.

"When the flesh gives, it's ripe," she said. She was smiling. She was holding it in her hand.

He felt the metal handles of the basket, grooves in his palm.

꜁

He got home. He pulled off his boots. He tried to find somewhere to put them. They smelled, his boots. He wanted to put them someplace. He couldn't find a place to put them. He left them in the back hall. He started to pull off his sweater. He got stuck in the middle. His nose scratched the old wool, his eyes pressed into stretched light, the space between shadows of fabric, this sweater really smells, he thought. All around him, nothing. His head in the sweater. A silence trapped in the noise of the day. Next door, someone said: "If you don't get into the shower right now I'm gonna kill you." He got the sweater off. He took a deep breath. The stench of boots.

The next time he thinks he is falling he closes his eyes and tries to just plummet.

Bottom, he keeps thinking, and the way he thinks that word, as if the bottom is a soft chair with arms to hold him while he slumps.

The black behind his eyelids: After images, moments that had happened, moments that were, horribly, irretrievably, happening.

The Two of Them

Rena said: "You think you can't, and then you can't." It was really a question about the inevitable. That was after the surgery, but before they knew he would get better.

Rena said she was going to leave and Morts said:

"No, don't leave, where are you going? Please don't leave."

He knew she was just going to work. She was only going to work.

She said: "Quit being a baby."

She said: "Stop it right now."

He was still in the bed. He could not get out of the bed. He felt the covers on him like a thick skin. He had healed by then. It was the first time she spoke to him that way. After she left, he touched himself under the sheets. The silence was hard, horrible.

He had always thought he was a man of action. But they lived enormous lives, lives spread across the possible distance.

She came back.

"If we get married, I'll die," he said. She looked at him with her huge brown eyes, specks of green out of the earth. Her pupils orbited. He thought: It's true. Then the moment of triumph. It's true.

What gave him the idea that they would marry? Rena, meanwhile, knew that she could leave at any time. People are always leaving. Her mother used to tell her father, even after they had been married for twenty years, 'You watch out. One day I'll just pick up and leave'.

Morts joked about her closet full of sweaters, but

Rena knew they were meaningless garments woven together by poor women in other countries.

Morts liked the idea of playing hockey more than he actually liked playing hockey. When he talked about getting the boys together to play some hockey, Rena nodded cheerfully and thought: This is our life.

Is it so horrible, to think: This is my life?

Morts was a man who did not know what to do with his body. Rena wondered if she should see someone, just to tell them what she was thinking about. But they didn't believe in that, the two of them. She went to her gynecologist for a check-up.

"I'm depressed," she said.

"I am too," her gynecologist said. For some reason, this was a story she felt she could tell Morts. She told him and he was nice to her for the entire weekend.

They lived in a house converted into three apartments. They lived in one of the apartments. It was very quiet when no one was home.

We eat ourselves up, Rena thought, looking at him that time when all he could do was drool. We have our real lives inside us. We feed our bodies to our real lives.

"Will we still fuck when we're eighty?" Morts said, the restaurant around them like a dream. He gulped from a bottle of beer. "The thing is," he said, "is that I don't want to be buried next to you. I don't know why. I just don't."

Let Me Show You To Your Seat

He was drowning. I'm drowning.

There were mirrors.

On the way down the stairs he was thinking about the train, about the subway going North. He was thinking about the subway so hard he ran into the mirror on the wall. His only vision was of himself.

He walked by his house. He had to stop on the corner and think about things. Already, he was questioning himself, thinking: Hey wait a minute – What about when we get old? What about that?

The knees are next to him.

When he licks the first time they are glossy and prescribed. Things must be protected from the air by a thin sheet of fabric tight on the bone. Also such things should consider a certain resistance to mucus and the warm seep of abundant fluids. At the theater he is sitting next to her, and her knees are making up the story. Oh god if the knees could be close together or spread far apart instead of this endless sense of timing, a space, a gap between her knees – he wanted to touch it, but it was nothing. He isn't very efficient himself. He knows about gaps. She thanks me for something I never did. The tickets, I got them for free from someone, I told her I bought them for us.

All through the performance I was drowning. I grabbed for a leg, felt the lump of her knee and slipped off the gentle bend.

How come you always want to do it after we eat? she said. I need to digest after we eat.

It's not swimming, he snapped.

Well maybe it is, she said.

Don't let go of her hand, someone said.

The phone was ringing, disturbing the performance. The knees, the beautiful knees. A plot is a series of lies arranged in conducive order. He spent three days afraid to open his eyes. In the crowded rows of seats he was squeezed between people – knees, he kept thinking, feeling the bend and sway. He was horrified by people. People might talk to him. Suddenly he went cross-eyed. There were twice as many people in the room. None of them whole. Excuses, he said. Pardons. They made room for him to leave, but not to get back in. He had to push. Another time, he saw spots for an entire day. They spread around the peripheral edges of his vision, drapes of light breaking through the brackish green of a lonely pond. He kept his eyes closed not thinking about what might happen if the phone suddenly rang or if he went to open up when he was already at the bottom.

I wanted her so bad I had to pretend not to know her. The play refused to end. He had nowhere to put his hands. His arms stuck out at angles. An uncomfortable shift. They say it takes years to fully adjust. Is this my date? You can only be as desperate as your itinerary.

He said things he regretted, whispering into her ear in the middle of the performance. She shifted away and refused to listen. He tried to put his arm on her armrest, thinking there was room on the padded blue velvet for both their arms to be side by side. The full length of his white pressed shirt pushed against the changing colour of her sleeveless limb. Her arms were naked. She crossed them across her body. The knees pressed together, exclamation points punctuating what he was trying to say. It's going to hurt he kept insisting, or it might have been her to him. Over and over again, whoever it was. They were in group session. There were only the two of them. It's going to hurt. Just the two of them. It's really going to hurt. When the spine is soft they give you something for the pain, then sample your fluids with a hot water tap. They give you something for the pain, she says, but it doesn't do a whole lot. It's going to hurt? he asks. He throws himself into the water. The last thing he sees are her knees, pointed twins gleaming in the night sky.

The phone still ringing.

We don't have to, he says.

But you want to, she says.

Not if you don't, he says.

You could just come over, she says.

But if I – But I would want to, he says.

It's okay.

No, no it isn't. I'll want to do it. I don't want to do it if you don't want to do it. You don't sound like you want to do it.

I do now, she says.

Really?

Yes really. All this talking about it...

Well I'll come over.

Come over.

You're sure?

Is it going to hurt?

He said he wanted to now but she said I have to go to the library maybe after when I get back from the library.

He thought if he sucked her breasts, which were bigger than usual. So he did and then she put her breasts back inside and got her coat.

Finally, then, he slipped down into the crack of his seat. He watched the proceedings. The play was a famous one. Everybody knew the story. The main characters were the woman and the gas furnace.

The phone in his pocket is ringing. People are looking around. He stares boldly ahead, leaning his body forward as if to catch the dialogue over the sound of this inconsiderate bleat. People around him touch sharp objects they keep handy. Extra large bobby pins, metal combs with spikes, retractable toothpicks. He leans further forward. Knees touching. The sound of shifting blades.

Angela: Hello? Hello? Who are you? Why are you calling me? What do you want? What do you want from me? Do you want me? Are you watching me? I know you're watching me. If you want me, you can have me. Anything. Just stop calling. Here! (Angela rips open her shirt.) Do you like them? Come and get them. Who are you? Is this what you want? Is this it? Do you like this?

He notices certain deviations from the original text. In the original, Angela does not bare her breasts. Rather, she pulls at her skirt and offers her rear portions. In the original, her tormentor, the gas furnace, responds quite gentlemanly and explains his predicament in the kind, upper class accent he picked up from his last owners, a fading dynasty of former plantation purveyors who rarely required his services on account of their Southern locale.

This is a modern version, he whispers to her, disgusted. Her seat is empty.

In this modern reenactment the furnace has to gradually acquire language. He calls and calls, but cannot communicate his need – more gas – until it is too late and he is already deeply and tragically in love with Angela. The furnace's side of the conversation is recreated by recordings of actual gas furnaces going on and off. He finds these dialogues disarming. The long creaks and groans of the hot desperate metal sound to him like the slow shuffle of a dying old man. Where is she? The gentleman sitting in front of him flicks open a straight razor.

She's missing the best part, he says.

Quiet!

She's missing the best part.

He cries at the sad parts. He cries when the gas

furnace reveals in his torturous bass vibrato of furniture shifts and winter rhythms that he started calling her because her number had once long ago been the number of the gas company. The furnace was designed to call the gas company automatically as soon as he went empty. For years he had been calling, never getting an answer. It was automatic. After he heard her voice, the voice of fuel, the plaintive hysteria of warmth – well his was a grilled sweet sheet metal heart, but did that mean he couldn't love? Even though he had only called to get more gas, he fell in love, and his calls became more than desperate notices that service was required. Oh god, Angela cries, sinking to her knees, rending her clothes to reveal both her bosoms and her bottom as she twirls in the agony of revelation, yes! yes! She also loves the gas furnace.

He was drowning.

How about staying down there until I'm finished?

He was trying to put it in.

She tightened her legs.

He looked at her, her legs locked around his body.

How about that?

He picked a hair off his tongue.

Someone was trying to contact him. To think, out of all these people, someone was trying to contact him. He dropped the phone.

Bravo! Magnifico! Encore! they yelled. He felt proud. The phone sent up ripples. He supposed he was drowning, because he thought of his mother, the way she used to touch him in the afternoon when he was a baby. He grabbed the phone long after it stopped ringing. Then, as if in a cartoon, he realized that he was drowning.

The Curator

In my own private collection there is no way to call. You are extending the boundaries. I pull out.

The volume is on the sun. Every time someone tries to get me on another line the wires melt.

This is not science. The leaves on my desk are left over from Fall. They sit in a jar.

It is, I almost always feel, the aspect of things that is incorrectly interpreted.

Packages arrive and I store them away. You are suspicious. You wait by the loading dock. You have every right to be suspicious. They aren't for me. I don't think they are for me.

Charleene

Charleene sticks her hand into the small white paper bag on her desk, pulls out a chocolate croissant. She takes a bite and chews. She has the same thing every morning.

Hodgins is supposed to fax London first thing before it is too late and everyone in London has gone home. He is supposed to make sure the fax goes through to London, then write down in the fax logbook, 'one fax to London,' and the fax number in London. He flips open the newspaper. He is an hourly worker.

"I used to be fat," he says.

"Really," Charleene says.

"Yes," Hodgins says. "Over two hundred pounds."

Charleene pops the last piece of croissant in her mouth.

She crumples her croissant bag into a ball. She throws the ball into the garbage. Hodgins gets out of his chair. Walks toward her. Puts his hands on her desk. Leans his face in close to hers. Nothing in her face is an indication. You're very committed to keeping in shape. I hate to work out. I never work out. Even as a little boy I never broke into a sweat. But you, well you're probably a natural. A real go-getter. And what perseverance. Hodgins pushes his body against her desk. They are fattening you up for the slaughter, all that muscle and tone and just the right thin layer of blubber.

Charleene's lips twitch.

It won't even hurt.

"What won't hurt?" Charleene whispers.

"That's what they said to me," Hodgins says.

"That's what they told me when they stuck their needles into me and pushed me into their machines and starved me. I was only a boy. I was eleven. It was glands in the end."

Charleene exhales. Her breath is sweet. She moves her teeth over her lower lip and bites down gently. Hodgins keeps himself very still. Charleene reaches toward his hand. She pats it.

"It's past the hour," she says, moving the stapler out of his shadow.

Fan

Mott switched off the television.

"Well I'm staying," he said.

"Great," Jer said. "I told you to stay."

"I guess I'm stuck here," Mott said. He put himself down on the floor in front of the fan.

"I was with Kerry last week –"

"You were with Kerry?"

"Yeah."

"Last week?"

"Yeah. She was driving."

"Kerry was driving?"

"Yeah."

"In her pick-up?"

"Yeah."

Mott sat up. He stuck his head in the fan.

"She's got a new boyfriend," he said. "A guy in a band. They've been at it for months. You should just forget her."

Jer got out of the beanbag chair. He fell back into it.

"What happened?" he said.

"Nothing. They're still together."

"No. When you were with her."

"Only that a huge beetle came flying through the window of the truck and hit me on my glasses. It was a huge fucking beetle. There was a crack. I yelled. And Kerry screamed –"

"Kerry screamed?"

"Yeah."

"You're full of shit."

"No, she screamed. I thought my glasses were

broken. It was huge. Left a wad of guts all over the lens. We dug it out of her purse. It was dead. Biggest thing I ever saw. I shoulda saved it."

"I thought it was dead," Jer said.

"What?"

"How could you save it?"

.   "Christ," Mott said. "Any beer left?"

Mott got up off the floor. He went over to the refrigerator.

"Bacon?" Mott said.

"You're not cooking bacon," Jer said.

Mott slurped his beer. The pan sizzled.

"Relax," he said.

"Get out," Jer said.

Mott laughed.

"It's too hot," Jer said.

"What's it matter? Ninety-eight degrees. A hundred degrees. Have a beer. Who cares?"

"We'll die," Jer said. "I'll die."

"Take off your shirt," Mott suggested.

Jer felt the skin around him. There was nothing to hold on to. He patted down the air.

"I'm thinking about a sandwich," Mott said. "You want a bacon sandwich?"

Jer moved to the window. He snapped the blind down and it rolled away from him, curling into itself.

"The sun is setting," he said. He looked down at his feet. Mott poked at the bacon with a fork.

"Sun down," Jer said.

Why not sleep? Why not wake up and feel the way you feel after sleep? Jer could smell the evening heat. He lifted his head. What had happened to the day? A damp patch of moisture on his chin. He wiped the wet drool with the back of his hand. He took another sniff at the night.

Mott was watching Star Trek.

The night was definite.

"Look who's awake," Mott said. He kept watching Star Trek. "I did the fucking pan."

The pan sat on the back burner, a stain of bacon grease glued to its scratched surface.

"It'll be cooler tomorrow," Jer said.

Mott nodded.

"Walk-out will be over," he said. "I'll be outta here. Trains'll be running. Fucking strike."

"I already told you to go, hours ago I told you," Jer said.

"Look," Mott said. "Captain's getting laid."

"Any beer left?" Jer said.

"A couple, maybe."

A woman with blue dots on both cheeks. The Captain lingered, pressed into flesh. Jer got out of the beanbag chair. The Captain pulled away from the embrace. Jer opened the refrigerator.

"You drank the whole six-pack," Jer said.

"Almost," Mott said.

"Drink water," Jer said.

"Fuck off," Mott said.

Jer held the beer.

"Can I ask you something?"

"Sure," Mott said. "Can I have that beer?"

Jer handed Mott the last beer.

"You're not having one?" Mott said.

Jer went back to the refrigerator. He looked inside.

"To the hottest day ever," he said.

Mott belched.

"So whaddaya wanna ask me?" he said.

"Nothing."

With Our Hands On Our Heads

This was last night:

She told me not to bike, but I biked. She was curled up in the blankets. She thinks too much, her worries all compressed into possibilities, the tight lines on her forehead, the innocent crest of her lips.

Her breasts swing loose. It's a show. I fall into her. I fall on her.

I thought you were going out, she said.

We always seem to be falling.

Swaying home, 2 am.

Her position, eliminated.

Well at least, I explain.

Whoever's smoking pot, says the waiter. If I catch you, you're outta here. Fitted white t-shirt. Tight black plastic shine pants with zippers running vertical over his thighs. Someone giggles. Pass it over here, the bass player says. The band kicks in, a Tom Waits song. I pick up a glass of beer.

Chokrin: I can't make it here.

Chokrin: I'm moving back to New York.

Chokrin: Art is dead here.

Chokrin: Everything is dead.

Around us, a frozen tableau of immobile hipsters, their flapping tongues crusting saliva dry. Where are we. That's all we know. Tight pants picks up my glass. I stick my hand in the air, two fingers out of a curl. He nods.

Chokrin: I'm going back. I've decided.

Chokrin: You come too.

Going home, swaying, yelling something that

sounds like a Tom Waits songs even though it isn't. I hit an iceberg in the middle of Queen Street.

Sixteen shells from a 30-Ought 6, the singer whispers. Drummer's wearing a toque that goes from the top of his head to his shoulders.

If you think anyone understands, I say.

What? Chokrin says. We're both yelling.

Forget it, I say.

All this? Forget all this?

She's asleep and I do my best to be quiet, my twisted bike, my boots, the sprawling jointage of my bruised limbs. Can't help falling into you. Can't help going to sleep and waking up next to you. You're right of course. You always are.

Wipe out.

And anyway, with my beer breath and cigarette hair, with my alcohol skin, with my dreams on me – loose, vaporous, veiled. She's asleep despite everything. Her position: a ball of curls, an apartment we call home.

After the first round, I buy all the drinks.

Busboy, labourer, envelope stuffer, van driver, data coordinator.

His hands on his head. He's broke.

There's nothing here for me. (Chokrin.)

Here? I say. Here?

That band seems to be playing the whole *Swordfish Trombones* album.

Bold, someone slurs.

Here? Here? Here?

Thin strip cords. Boots. Thick gray socks. Striped button down shirts, fifties style.

And when we're old and fat?

I don't know from cool. I don't believe in cool. (Chokrin?)

I have this idea about someone who has all these

ideas but no money. Money=ideas. Do I have to make you understand everything? This is what comes in the mail: We can't understand everything. We can't make this work. We like your idea. But we can't –

the

public.

Canada, Chokrin says. I was doing better in New York.

Just a place, I snap. Like every place.

The two of us, we have this theory about luck. When it comes your way you have to wrassle with it, it'll be bucking, it's some kind of greasy beast. You get it around the neck, hold on for your life and before you know it you're sliding off its haunched rear, your hands just slipping through the fronds of luck's tail. And then you're back in the dirt again, waiting – hoping – for another ride.

Only our graduation dates are different. Otherwise, we are all the same. Pick us up off the floor of the club's back room where the band plays live Tom Waits funeral dirges. Position us just so. With our hands around our glasses. With our eyes wide open. For realism, someone has stuck a burning cigarette in Chokrin's lips. I watch in paralytic horror as the stub burns down, the stink of blistering, put a piece of liver over it someone suggests. I know what they're thinking. I account for my organs. Flashbulbs, vid-cams, circumstance. Someone's getting famous. Someone's capturing the moment. The –

Public.

How can they do that? I say. How can they?

Well, she says. They did it.

Those fuckers.

They might close the whole hospital, she says.

I follow her into the kitchen. She's in her work clothes, reserved dresses, long skirts – Oh the creases! Oh the conservative finery!

Look, I explain. I didn't get a chance to do them.

You always say you'll do them but then you never do them.

She stands where she is. Arms crossed. We stare into the sink, the pile of dishes a lurking wild beast, crusted forks jutting out like quills. (I was –

waiting for a call. I was –

hoping against hope. I was –

riding luck's lucky beast.)

Too dirty, I mutter. Needed to soak. (My position – spiraling down the drain – so much dirty water – eliminated.)

I can remember as far back as last week. That was the week they banned smoking in all public places. Hipster outcry ignored. Chokrin's long artist fingers are sideways stained. He's not the only one puffing away. Anarchy? Victory? Stupidity? The waiter doesn't care, some fines are just the cost of doing business. Above our heads great gaseous clouds of smoke hover, first looming, then threatening, then encompassing everything.

Waiter! I hold up two fingers. I punch a hole in the fog. I tip one dollar.

After the first round, I paid for everything.

(Go, she said. I don't mind.)

I had to borrow just to buy a few fucking groceries, Chokrin says. Two degrees and I can't get a fucking job in this city. My luck, my luck

is

smoking.

(Just don't buy him drinks. You always spend all your money buying him drinks.)

Fine, go, I say. I don't mind.

She's my only true love, croons the singer. The drummer's toque has slipped over his torso, he's wiggling, imprisoned, keeping time by crashing his head into the cymbal. It's a slow song.

Made in Canada, I say.

He says: My application was due, so I ducked into the pub to have a quick pint and look everything over. At the last minute, I changed my mind and applied for the lower grant, a thousand dollars instead of five. Pathetic. I changed my mind. I figured that at least this way I'll have a fucking chance...

He nods while he talks, agreeing with himself, encouraging me to drink up –

Weaving my bicycle. Shouting something I know to be singing. On my way.

Fuck grants, he says. When was the last time someone any good got a fucking grant?

She takes these pills to keep it going. Her heart beats louder and harder. In the afternoons, she guides the kid through the tests. Then she calls me:

Poor kid, can barely speak, I had to skip the second battery. Poor little guy.

Get out of my way, I say. I'm not even looking. My eyes are shut.

Chokrin: Oh shit look over there. Remember that guy? (This guy we knew from university – lining up to graduate, shiny paper caps lying gingerly on our palms, two hundred and twenty-five dollar graduation fee already deducted, cap and gown included, included, absolutely included. Later, when he's gone, Chokrin tells the story of his New York Master's degree graduation, how his brother came up to witness the event, how they both got so drunk the night before neither of them could make it to the ceremony...)

Chokrin: Shit he sees us.

Squirrels over, peers in our direction, his eyes PH D bright. He's wearing: sneakers, faded Gap jeans, a sweater (brown [academic]). He's drinking a bottle of Carlsberg. Light.

Chokrin: How ya doin'?

(He's just finishing up. After that, who knows?... A teaching job, probably somewhere in the States.)

The phone rings. I jolt into the hardware of it, planes crashing, cars revving, ambulances running red lights, bikes folding into pavement.

This was last night: Kneeling in front of the fridge, rice in a shaking spoon, my mouth a round dark trough, farts out of me in oval squats.

Bowel

I have not changed the world.

On the way home I passed over a river. I stood in the middle of the silent bridge and held the book out over the water and felt a slipping between my thumb and forefinger.

When she looked at me, with her arms narrowed and her eyes obvious, I gave her the book.

"Here," I said, "I got you something."

"Oh," she said. "Where did you get this?"

"A place," I said. "Just this place."

I put my arms around her and told her I loved her.

"I love you," I said. I cried a little. I cried for the stranger getting married. I cried for my marriage. Which way was the way home? I had this feeling things had changed. I took the book out of her hands, read the first few sentences out loud. The kitchen was bright. The words meant nothing to me.

"I wrote this book," I told her.

She was beautiful. I still think about her.

Barbecue

"I'm afraid of it," Babs said.

She stood on the other side of the deck, her arms crossed, her back against the warped wooden wall. Behind her, below her, the alley between their new apartment and the dry cleaning business.

Don't lean, Junior thought, staring just past her head into the weak spring sun.

"So why did they leave it," Babs said. "If there's nothing wrong with it, why did they leave it?"

"Take it easy," Junior said. He crossed the deck, knelt in front of the small barbecue.

"You're not going to touch it?" Babs asked.

Junior flipped open the lid.

"I'm going inside," Babs said.

"Go," Junior agreed. "Go."

"What?" she was yelling. "What did you say?"

Junior felt her voice sail into the sky, a fluttering bird perched on the deck, taking off again.

"Nothing."

"I hope it was nothing."

He peered into the barbecue. The grill was rusted, the coals were gray speckled dandruff white. It's just a barbecue, he thought.

"I'm really scared of it," Babs whispered. Junior turned. Arms tight into each other, legs prickling in the cool wind, back hard against the weathered planks. He imagined going to her, pulling her against the safe slant of his chest, saying, I'm here, it's okay now.

He crouched closer. Dug into his shirt pocket. Pulled out his lighter.

Postage

Dear –,
It rained. It poured. It hailed. I made coffee. May, 1997.
June, 1997. August, 1997. I made married. I counted my
monetary gaps. Divorced. I filed my name like a business. The phone doesn't ring. I won't panic, I won't even
think: AC payments, the cost of having beer delivered,
cold showers, keeping cool. The guy living downstairs
is a chef. He leaves everyday of the week at 10:35 am.
The door swing shuts. I stay where I am. The guy
upstairs is some kind of mechanic. He leaves at 6:30,
comes back at 4:15. He's been living here for eight
months now. I've never seen him. I go out the front. I
remember something I thought I'd forgotten. I march
back up the stairs, unlock the door and take a seat at
my desk. The papers on either side of the computer are
the documents I promise to subscribe into the machine,
enter and discard and print out again – everything:
filed, recorded, saved, soiled, uploaded, reborn, re-
birthed. You bastard. Don't start this crazy shit again.
PK Dick, Dalton Trumbo, Vonnegut. Try reading something short and blunt like a fist. Summer hail. Sun goes.
Love –.

Dear –,
You write me a postcard. You write me a letter. You write
me an email; Subject: This is the summer of going crazy.
Getting email is like getting a letter except you don't
think about it, you don't value it, you don't feel like you
should keep it before you throw it out. Instead, you
respond immediately and you don't remember what

you said and you figure, well, anyway, someone somewhere is keeping a record, has a kilobyte file with your
name on it, is storing up everything you've already
forgotten. So why should I?
Wishing You the Best, –.

Dear –,
When was it? A few summers ago? A few hot decades
interspersed with this tiresome cold season? I drank
beer by the lakeside and said later: So I'm heading out
for a midnight canoe ride. You called me crazy, called
me irresponsible, tried to take my beer away. I laughed
and said you're so gullible. Just kidding, I said. My hot
body. My ha ha ha. My message in a sinking bottle.
Salutations, –.

Dear –,
I have lost a crucial invoice, a bill I thought I paid, a
dream in crayon on a pink piece of recycled scrap. I
clean the desk and find the letter I received from you
five months ago. I feel guilty the way those men who go
to Thailand to have sex with little boys feel guilty. I
forget what I am looking for. I forget everything. I write
back. Not word for word but subject for subject, idea for
idea, my heart, my breast, my clinging flesh to flesh.
Hope All Is Well, –.

Dear –,
Winter's only over and you're already burning through
summer like a forest fire set by an errant American
outdoorsman who just can't face the darkness, who
promised his Sherrie a big bon in the big outdoors. Don't
come visit. I got bills to pay and a headache this big.
Best –.

Dear –,
You send me this story by Harlan Ellison about a man

who keeps bumping into his ex-wives and having sex with them, one night stands full of regret and longing and bitterness like the skin of a fruit. I stop reading it. I swallow. He has eight ex-wives, and he notices a pattern by the third most recent wife. Here's the catch: his first wife, numero uno wife, wife number one, his original true love. Fifty-four per cent of all first marriages are failures.

Hugs and Kisses, –.

Dear –,

Dandruff like it's never been seen before. If you didn't write me, I wouldn't feel compelled to write you back. Shaking my head over a piece of paper. You've noticed that I almost never respond to your emails. And when was the last time I sent *you* a postcard of a tanned woman in a white bikini with the name of a state written under her in bright letters? Georgia, Florida, Oklahoma. Coincidentally, I'm sure, these are the names of your daughters. I cannot help you find them, we are no longer in contact. Though I will say they are all fine women, tall and clear complexioned with strong minds. Invoice number: 935-1. 4-Apr-97. 2000 covers printed two colours over one colour varnished. Prepress 81. Paper 100. Print/bind 260. GST 35.07. PST 0. Found this bill next to your scribbles. You see, I do keep records. Enclosed please find a copy of my recent catalogue, no obligation necessary. You don't know how busy I am. I'm taking some time out of my day-to-day. You think business slumps in the summer? Here, it's the other way around. Try to keep cool. Try to read less speculative adult fiction. Try to imagine yourself before dignity's veil cast over your face like mist rising in a morning's wilderness only partially spoiled by motor boats. A morning that nobody knows.

All the Best, –.

Dear –,
Extra Blue Selsun strong with medicated tingle. Tea tree oil Koala All Natural Antibacterial Exfoliate. I buy hot oil cleansing scalp unclog treatment. I stay up late soaking my hair in an old wive's tale of oatmeal, dark ale and maple syrup. I see a commercial for Nizoral, kills the fungus that starts dandruff, $15.99 for a small bottle that fits in my palm, two teaspoons twice a week. This is how I live now – do not ingest, do not leave near children, product as magic, guaranteed write McNeil Laboratories, Guelph, Ontario for a full conditional refund details of offer available. Fungus. Fungus.
Missing ya, –.

Dear –,
Your postmarks from Florida. Your special deliveries from Idaho. Your warning from the post master associate of upstate New York: postage due, six cents. But they deliver it anyway and that's something, isn't it? Remember me, you write from your cell in Pittsburgh. Your jail in Pennsylvania. Pittsburgh. I say it out loud. I feel hot breath on my butt. Pittsburgh. Your legs pulling around my chest. Jail. The way he pins me down from a distance. The way he licks my anus like a stamp.
Regretfully Yours, –.

Smell It

She lets him put in as many as he wants. There are wind chimes and mobiles everywhere, surrounding the bed, hanging off the walls like ivy. He thinks he will stick his nose in and see if he can smell her. When he tries to lower himself down her flesh, everything jingles. She closes her legs, drawing him back up. She rubs his parts indiscriminately. There is enough of the night.

"I like you," she says.

He crawls around on top of her.

"I'm not on the pill," she says.

He puts his tongue in her mouth, drools.

Later there will be a walk. The rain will be a mist – something he cannot quite put a finger on.

There was a woman who loved him, he thought to tell the olfactory expert. She smelled clean. She smelled like baby powder. There was a woman.

"Look at this," a doctor said, large, clear nostrils flaring. "What do you see?"

Hans saw an internal reflection, grays and blacks, shadows. He turned away. Now he knew a face could be reduced to an echo. He shuddered and sought to repeat himself.

It occurred to him – when it was, as they often say, too late – that he should stop thinking everything was funny. The for sale sign on the front lawn did not go away. He went outside to confirm this observation. Yes, there it was, tottering acrobatically, barely jabbed into the ground.

They were supposed to care about you.

Hans referred to his convictions. He leaned on the sign. Something white fell from his torso. It was becoming necessary to carry tissues, to wear only shirts with pockets.

"What are you doing?"

Even upwind of her, he scented nobody. As if she wasn't there.

"What is he doing?" she asked the babies.

Hans tried to get off the sign. He thought he was changing.

"Stop that," she said.

"Put the sign back," she said.

"I have to get back to the daycare," she said.

"We have to get back, don't we?" she said, picking up the hand of a baby and flapping it.

"Goodbye," she said. "Say goodbye."

Eager to learn, all the babies flapped their limbs. The grass, soft under the hard sign, let him know his body.

The situation had gotten unbearable. He thought the subject of study was himself, his problem, his nose.

She rolls up to him, circling the tarmac, flashing blinkers suggesting permission for take off. Hans is afraid of flying, but he does not protest. He should have said: "I am breathing through my mouth."

He touches her, exploring his own hands, how they are changing.

After that there were phone calls he wasn't sure he was making. Silence over invisible lines. He could hear himself swallow through the process of imagining an imaginary scent.

He carried the portable into the bathroom and masturbated. The hum of the fan and panting frenzy of his breath distracted him. He thought he would have to pay for the call. He figured things were getting more and more expensive. He wiped up with a rag.

There was a woman.
He thought they had already been through that.
"Lie back and breathe," he heard the doctor say.

The Summer

Flutter and die. Decrepit wings between us. Wipe the dust off our faces. Turn away from the season.

Over here where I am, the moths bang across the screen.

In winter it is too cold to follow the sidewalk.

Hey, whose face is that? Eyes closed to the cold. I see nose, lips, the flash of a white cheek. I see what peaks out from the pink of a doubled-up parka.

The months are nothing: days, heats, feelings.

Parcel Check

James spits into his radio. "I need some help here," he yells.

I can hear the splatter. The girl in the red blouse laughs. James runs down the aisles. I take a drink.

"Who's that?" the girl asks. I shrug and burp.

"Am I coming through?" James yells.

I pass the girl the bottle. I pick at the side of my nose. She's fat, but not so fat. James gasps into his radio. I unbuckle my belt. The radio pulls my pants down. I tug the belt out of the loops in my pants. The radio slips through and falls. I pick it up and put it on an empty cardboard box.

"There's a huge line at parcel check," James yells. The box shakes.

"He used to be in the army," I say to the girl. She puts her mouth back, drinks with her neck. I do that thing with my eyebrows. The girl rolls her eyes.

"Don't drink all that," I say. Her blouse is open in bulges. "Save some room."

A Long Day With Goldberg

Goldberg comes back from checking the bathrooms and smoking a joint. We go out the rear doors and sit on the concrete, our backs against the faded bricks of the trade centre. Our red security jackets are made of felt and plastic.

"It's hot," I say. Goldberg giggles. My jacket sticks to my skin. Behind us, the door slams. Goldberg doesn't flinch. I press against the wall. A woman rounds the corner, stops, stares over at us.

We are under the sun. Cars break past. Spring blows gently off the trap of Lake Ontario. I feel air on my face. Goldberg giggles quietly.

"What?" the woman says.

I close my eyes and tilt my head up to the sun. Goldberg makes a crooning out of the corner of his mouth. I love Goldberg at the end of the day. The faint scent of hash stuck in his bristly hair, his fat nose wavering under his unfocused pupils. Yeah, I love Goldberg.

The orange under my eyes turns. I look carefully through slits. The woman has a long thin shadow that cuts through the sun, the wind, the brush of passing traffic. I smile at her. Me and Goldberg, we make nine dollars every hour. We are on the job.

Alien

"You held my hand," Persky's brother said.

Persky's hands were fists hanging just apart from his body.

"You did," his brother said.

"Well," Persky said. "I know what you don't know."

"What's that?" Persky's brother said. Persky's brother was a lawyer in training.

"I know how she died," Persky said.

Persky's brother smiled. "How's that?" he said.

Persky shrugged.

"Tell me," Persky's brother said. "Tell me already."

Persky just stood there, smiling, swinging his arms, his soft hands shaking in fists blunt through the apartment air.

"Fine then," Persky's brother said. "Don't tell me."

"She died because of the aliens," Persky said. He was whispering. "They landed on her house. Because she was a survivor."

Persky's brother got mad. He punched Persky in the shoulder, hard. "What's wrong with you?" he said.

Big Luba was making soup. The soup she made was always perfect. Big Luba had perfected her soup over the long years, each year she lived seemed longer. Actually, she had perfected her soup almost fifty years ago. She was eighty-two. She perfected her soup the year her husband died of a heart attack. That was the year they could afford a chicken every week.

Big Luba made her soup very clear. It was never greasy. When people drank her soup they said: "Big

Luba, your soup! It's so clear! It's not greasy! How do you do it?" Big Luba wasn't afraid of revealing the secret of her soup. She told the secret to her daughter, her two daughters-in-law and the one grandchild who called every week. She told them her secret, but they did not make the clear chicken soup.

Big Luba poured the extra soup she made in a Belle Belle margarine container. She always made more soup than she herself could drink. The excess soup was for her grandchildren. Her grandchildren rarely visited. She opened the freezer. The freezer was full. There was no room on top of the stack of Belle Belle margarine containers already in the freezer. This stack of containers went all the way up to the top where the ice was layering. She needed to defrost the freezer, but she had nowhere to put all the margarine containers. The next time one of her children visited, she would give them some frozen soup to take home for her grandchildren. When would that be? The freezer was full. There was also in the freezer fourteen steaks. She kept steaks in case her sons came to see her. She bought steaks when they were on sale. Three chickens. Six veal chops. Two packages of ground chicken. One huge turkey wing. A lamb chop. No lamb, the doctor told her, but every once in a while.

The shelf of the freezer was occupied by a plastic grocery store bag filled with kreplach. Kreplach were Big Luba's specialty. No one made kreplach like Big Luba. Kreplach were dumplings filled with ground chicken meat. They were served floating in a bowl of soup as clear as one of those winter days when it was too cold for Big Luba to walk even to the Golden Age to play cards. What secret? Big Luba asked her daughter, her two daughters-in-law and the one grandchild who called every week. It's just hard work to make kreplach, Big Luba said. That's all. There's no secret. She told them the recipe. A bissle of this, a spoon of salt, and the dough, not too thin. But nobody made kreplach from her recipe. And lately, when Big Luba made kreplach, she felt this sinking in her stomach that didn't go away even after two white pills and one pink one. Rolling the dough took hours. Her fingers were tired. They were hard to move. She got sleepy and fell asleep in her chair in the kitchen. The blue bowl with the crack that didn't go all the way through was filled with dough waiting to be worked by her strong, tired fingers. Night fell. Weeks passed. The phone rang three times. One or two of her friends from the Golden Age dropped by to see why she hadn't come to play a few rounds of pinochle. They saw why: Big Luba up to her wrinkled elbows in flour and ground chicken. They left.

Persky thought: Those ties with the rips already in them, very strange. They come like that. The funeral home hands them out. They say – are you a mourner? and then if you say yes they give you a tie with a rip already ripped in it. So somebody rips the ties and then sews them up so that the mourners can rip them again. Steinman and Sons, that's what this place is called. I rode in the limo. I didn't trust the driver. Sounds like a kosher butcher. Steinman and Sons. They probably get their ties from China. Prison labour. Why not? You're not going to get me wearing one of those Chinese ties with the rip ripped and then sewn up so that I can rip it again.

She was standing in her kitchen holding the hot Belle Belle margarine container full of soup and looking at her full freezer when her house started to shake.

"Oy got," Big Luba said. Outside it was dark where minutes before – or had it been hours? – it had been so light. So what about this shaking? The soup was hot through the thin plastic in her hands. She didn't feel the heat. She was Big Luba, and after her funeral someone would tell the story of how she could take a piping hot pan of brisket out of the oven with her bare hands. She had given birth to her first son alone in Siberia. She had starved. She had been poor. She had watched them hang cousin Moishke in the square. She had waited for her grandchildren to call, she had escaped Poland with her husband, she had been nineteen and handsome. So she was going to waste soup, because of a little shaking and a full freezer? She took a spoon and put it in her apron pocket. Carefully, holding the hot Belle Belle margarine container in the grooved palm of one of her big hands and trailing the peeling wallpaper wall with the other, she moved down the hall. Thick red carpet rolled under her. She would drink the leftover soup in the basement.

Persky was picking at the dried skin on the cusp of his big toe.

He had the television on, but he wasn't watching.

He was making a list. He liked to make lists. He made numerous lists, each of which related to his other lists. For instance, he made a list of the foods he would need. Canned stuff, mostly. Then he made a list of the weaponry. Then he made a list of all the people he hated. Then he made a list of all the movies he had seen that concerned World War II. Then he made a list of all the movies he had seen that tangentially referred to World War II, neo-Nazis, and/or psychoanalysis. Persky realized that the lists he made were never complete. He was dependent on memory. He could not have expected the lists to be accurate. Still, Persky thought, I remember a lot. He made a note to himself on a note card. He made a fist around a pen. The phone rang.

"Persky?" It was his brother. Persky looked at his clock. He was expected at work in five hours and fourteen minutes. Persky was an usher. He marched people to their seats. He preferred the sold out events.

Techniques of bending. The quiet confidence of control. He took note of the nose sizes of regular concert-goers. He measured on his fingers. He recalled certain kinds of thick almost kinky hair.

"Persky?" Five hours and twelve minutes. "I know you're there."

"How?" Persky said. "How do you know I'm here?"

"I've got some bad news," Persky's brother said. "I've got bad news."

Some of the things said about Big Luba at her funeral were exaggerations. It was true that she persevered, that she was brave, that she was a survivor. It wasn't true that she was courageous. It was true that she was sharp-tongued, even witty. It wasn't true that she was bitter. It was true that she had had many brothers and sisters who died during the war between countries that had also been at war against her family and friends. But it wasn't true that she had had fifteen brothers and sisters who had all died in the death camp Treblinka. Actually, she had had twelve brothers and sisters. She whispered their names in the dark basement. Although she had no way of knowing, she knew that three of them were shot by the Poles, two were hung by the Germans, one of them killed herself on a boat overloaded with refugees, and the rest died in various death camps, terrified, alone. Big Luba shouted their names while the house shook. She held the Belle Belle margarine container in her lap. The faded green couch rattled in place. The alien ship landed on her small house and crushed it.

Four days after the funeral Persky left his parents' house in the company of his brother and his brother's wife. His brother was driving. Persky sat in the back seat. He was bent over himself, prepared for accidents or worse. At the first red light he unbuckled his seat belt and said: "Let me off here."

"Shut up," Persky's brother's wife said.

"Don't tell him to shut up," Persky's brother said. The light changed. The car accelerated. Persky thought of the list he would start: Reasons to be suspicious of my brother and his wife.

Persky's back was starting to hurt because of the way he had to sit, hunched up, curved into the cramped back of the Audi. They had been driving much longer than Persky had thought they were going to be driving.

"Why don't we go back," Persky suggested, voice muffled, face deep in his knees.

"Shut up," Persky's brother's wife said.

They were looking for the kosher deli. There was a certain meat product Persky's brother and Persky's brother's wife thought highly of that they could not get in their neighbourhood. Their neighbourhood had a kosher grocery store, but no kosher deli. The meat product in question was called kernatzel.

After some time, it became apparent that Persky's brother could not find the kosher deli.

"I demand to be taken back," Persky said, bravely poking his head up.

Persky's brother's wife looked out the window.

"You said you knew where it was," Persky's brother yelled, slamming his hands on the steering wheel. "You said it was this way."

Persky's brother executed a dramatic u-turn.

Persky's face between his knees, almost touching the thin car carpet.

"I'm sorry," Persky's brother said. "I didn't mean to yell."

Persky saw the point where their hands touched.

"Let's go back now," he said.

"Shut up," they said, but together and very gently.

The house squashed like a bug. It spread sideways, its guts bursting out from under the weight of the alien ship. The basement was fine, the walls were cracked, the occasional chunk of plaster fell off the ceiling, but mostly, the basement was fine. Big Luba sprayed her hair a hard shell every morning. The bigger chunks bounced off. The smaller chunks stuck. An alien landing could neither change the basement nor her hair. Both had remained immutable since her youngest son moved out. Big Luba had wanted her sons to be doctors. She had grudgingly settled for a dentist and a teacher.

Big Luba got up. She put the Belle Belle margarine container on the old dusty couch. She was careful to make sure that it was upright. She did not want any soup to spill past the lid. She made her way through the gloom over to the stairs. She walked slowly, but no slower than usual. Threads of light spun through small cracks. Big Luba climbed the stairs. The stairs got narrower and narrower until she had to stoop which was hard for her. And anyway, the stairs didn't lead to the door, the thick wood door was up above her head now, and the stairs ended in a cloistered enclosure. From what Big Luba could see, the space where the door used to be was now a thin passageway tangled by webs of sharp edges and wires. Maybe the passageway would have been big enough for her youngest grand-child to get through. But not Big Luba. Her youngest grandchild was six. His Bar Mitzvah was in seven years. He could not yet be blamed for anything. The stairs were the only way out of the basement.

Big Luba sat back down on the couch and waited. She waited ten days. Each day she drank two large spoonfuls of soup, and one small spoonful of soup. When the soup was gone and ten days had passed, she once again recited the names of her brothers and sisters. This time she added the names of her parents, her cousins and a few of the companions she had grown up with in Poland. Finally, she said to her husband the tailor: "So where are our children? That they would leave me here?" Big Luba and her husband had lived for four months in the American's refugee camp waiting to be sent to a country called Canada. She hadn't been unhappy then, they had slept together with the first baby between them on a thin cot. She hadn't been so unhappy, not then. Big Luba curled her fingers into fists. It hurt to make fists.

After the ten days had gone by and all the names had been recited, Big Luba thought things that she had never dared think before. A cloud of dust shook out of a crater in the ceiling, shrouding her hair. The alien ship prepared to take off. Big Luba's heart burst open. The Belle Belle margarine container fell off the couch. The spoon hit the warped basement tiles. An empty ringing.

At the funeral, Persky's father spoke. Then Persky's brother spoke. Persky stood next to his brother on the podium. He didn't speak. Persky's brother said:

"What would we give to sit at her table one more time?"

Persky realized he was crying. Persky's brother took his hand. Persky's hand was loose, open.

Bungalow

Nothing goes uneaten. My meals swallowed in a space beneath the sun. The beasts circle. I chew on strips of dried salted flesh. The truck comes. I give them what they want. They leave.

The inside of a large leathery egg can be eaten slowly with a spoon. Bury it in the sand for fifteen minutes. I hike to the top of the ridge and see the hiss of dust dragged behind the truck like a trailer. The road ends and they take what I have left and leave me what I want. When they are over the first hill I run down. Things circle and sniff. I run. A clicking brown animal drives its teeth into the package. I kill it with my hands.

Certain things can be forgotten. The scent of electricity. The taste of gasoline. I don't know what to say. There are things I haven't said. I set traps for campers. Motor homes are expendable. Go past the garden, a field of wilting cactuses in the sand. Veer in any direction. Garden gives way to ocean. At the ocean they dive in together. Sand floats down their throats. They swallow the taste of an old promise. I trace my hand along the white stone of my wall. This story is not over. They come in the morning. They walk on me. The baffle of feet is a sermon. I eat the sound.

Don't try and creep up on me. I'm warning you. Don't try it.

Hearth

As soon as she goes out he has his pants down.

The summer has a way of ending.

Next year he'd be an old man. He'd have to get a job mowing lawns. Mr. Lee the neighbour bending out of his house on his cane saying you boys miss so many spots here, here, here, here, the cane waving like summer heat.

Let me smell your hands.

He sticks out his hands. She has to bend down to smell them. His hands – an offering – wave under her body.

You, she says and grabs him by the wrists. She smells her lotion on his palms. She pulls his hands up hard. His elbows jam. He cries out. His toes jump up toward her. She is tall and soft.

You've been jerking off.

She bends over him, hits him once on each ear. Harder, he thinks, so that later he can let the hot blood collect slowly in the sunken curve of her belly.

Go outside and wait for the mail, she says. Mom's sent us a cheque.

How Could You

On the way to the store, Herb meets his girlfriend.

Do you think you'd know my pussy, if that's all you could see?

You would be able to recognize it, wouldn't you?

Well would you?

What if you could smell it?

And taste it?

What then?

Could you be sure?

How could you?

Herb watches his girlfriend walk away. His tongue slips out of his tight mouth and hangs there.

Usher

The children, all lined up on the big stage, their shy faces blushing and glowing under strings of Christmas bulbs. He thinks about their little throats opening, closing, singing and singing, all the words he has forgotten come back to him. He will hum along, the children in their red school jackets and blue pants, marching. He puts one foot out the door. Lowers himself carefully down the stairs. Already, he is tired. The children are scampering backstage, dancing and shoving and pushing and trying out the words.

He squints through his good eye, sticks his cane out, feels it dig through the crust of ice and slip. He swings his legs forward. Is he late? The cold is killing him. He tries to go very fast. The people – the many people – rush around him. He isn't even moving. I'm not dead yet. He feels dizzy. One boot in front of the other. When he turns the corner he sees the red circle, the neon words. Another year he made it all the way to see the children. The night is rubber, his legs melt. He is halfway stuck when the light changes. A taxi edges forward trapping him. Good, let him try and run me over. When my son gets here – well let him. I'm old anyway. He makes it over the curb, laughing out loud, I'm not that old, the tears out of his blind eye thick, sticky.

Ticket please.

The girl holds her hand out.

Behind her he can see the lovely lobby lit up and decorated. The girl is smart in her red bow tie and vest.

I've come to see the children.

You need a ticket, she says.

There are people behind him. A crowd. Pushing.

I come every year, he tells her. With my wife. My boy, Joseph. Where is Joseph?

The box office, she says. Just outside and down to the end of the building. This way. She takes his elbow. She pushes him along a few steps. Tickets please, she yells, have your tickets ready.

Well where is he? The door opens fast and he holds on to it so he won't fall.

I've come to see the children, he says.

Can I help you? the boy says. Sir?

I've come to see the children.

He leans in at him, his nose almost touching the metal, his cane shaking.

Joseph, he says. You're late. We'll miss the children.

Tickets under Joseph? the boy asks. And your order number?

We're late now, he says. He isn't really worried. We're late.

Oh, the boy says, plenty of time before the show starts. Fifteen, twenty minutes.

Joseph, he breathes. His nose is running. He brings his hand up to his pocket. The gap in his jacket. A tight pocket, nothing there. His cane falls out in front of him.

Joseph, he says. Hand me my handkerchief.

I can't find any tickets for Joseph, the boy says.

He can't get the handkerchief out. It's gone. It's gone, he says, surprised. Gone. And then looking through the grille and seeing the boy in there.

I have no reservation under Joseph.

He isn't Joseph. That boy in there, anyway, he isn't Joseph.

If you had the order number...

The children. I've come to see the children.

I'm afraid we have no record of your ticket sir. If you'll just...

The boy looks down at him from behind his metal sheathe.

I can give you something on the gallery. Is the gallery alright sir?

The children, he says.

The gallery then, the boy says. That's twenty-three ninety-six.

Joseph's late.

Sir?

I need Joseph, he says.

Sir, the boy says, if you'll just –

The boy picks up the blue ticket and holds it between his fingers. He looks at the old man.

If you'll just wait over there. He points to the other side of the room.

We're late already, he says. He takes an uncertain step. There is heat on his face. The heavy door swings open for him. He moves back around the corner. He sees the girl in red. The bright red smiling usher –

Please, he says to her, to the red, to the smiling usher.

I am not an usher, she says.

The Earth is an Anus

The Moon is covered in tall brown strands. Although there is no wind, this vegetation waves about in vaguely expressive gestures. Bob turned to Rob and asked, "Do you think they could be alive?"

"You mean like... sentient?" Rob replied.

"Yeah, like animals. Or people."

"Well," Rob said, slowly, "when we take some samples, we'll maybe find out."

"Okay, okay. But first, will you give me a kiss?"

Rob kissed Bob. Their lips touched lightly and Bob pulled Rob closer.

"Dammit Bob," Rob said, pulling away, "we're the first people to get to the moon and you want to screw?"

"C'mon Rob," Bob replied, "what better time?"

They sat on the ground holding hands, watching the sun drop out of sight.

Bob stroked the surface of the moon slowly. "You know," he said, "I think it's getting tighter. It seems less gushy, harder to slide around."

Rob patted a patch.

"When we got the mission," he said, "I had a hard time explaining it to my grandmother." Bob nodded. Rob's grandmother had died just a month before. "I said to her," Rob chuckled, "I said 'I'm going to the moon.' 'What kind of job is that?' she said. 'You to the moon? What place is this? For this they give you money?' So I took her outside, you know Bob, she was already quite sick, could barely walk. I helped her out to the porch and, as if I had planned it, there it was, hanging like a great pink golf ball in the night sky. 'Look Grandma,' I said. 'Look, that's the moon. That's where I'm going.'

"Grandma was very short, so for her it must have seemed even farther then it did for us. She shuffled about until she got a good look at the sky and then, it's weird, because it seemed like at last, for the first time, she was starting to understand, you know, who I was and what I was about. She turned around so she was looking at me and said, 'To the moon with that Bob?' 'Yeah, Grandma,' I said. 'To the moon with Bob.' And she went inside, laughing to herself, you know the way she did, and muttering 'To the moon with Bob, ah, to the moon with Bob... ' "

Rob fell silent, feeling the weight of Bob's hand on his and the moon's surface under his palm: wrinkled yet smooth, warm yet curiously cool. The silence seemed an almost unreal luxury after the constant humming of the Earth and the furor surrounding their departure. Bob broke it obliviously.

"I wonder," he said, "should we sleep outside, or in the ship?" Rob shrugged. They sat a little while longer, their gazes shifting from one brown strand to another as the waving pilose greetings competed with each other for attention.

"Outside," Bob said. "We belong outside."

They hiked across the great expanse of the moon. They were on their way to explore a small and slightly raised patch of brown terrain sporting a single strand standing erect in the exact centre of their destination. Bob had seen it from the roof of the shuttle which he had climbed that morning to have a look around.

"Hey Rob," Bob had said, "come look at this." Rob had abandoned his work and pulled himself through the hatch of the craft and up onto the roof.

"What?" Rob had asked.

"Look at that patch of brown over there."

"Where?"

"Just over there. Just lingering on the horizon." Bob pointed urgently and, when Rob stated that he still couldn't see it, Bob clutched Rob's chin and pushed Rob's gaze into line with his own.

"Over there," Rob exclaimed. "Why didn't you say so?"

"Yeah, and –"

"You shouldn't employ such imprecise terms. I mean, lingering? We *are* scientists. How am I supposed to understand that? Use degrees. You know? Like, thirty degrees to your left. There. I would have had it right away. How about that, Bob?" Rob spat off the tip of the shuttle, his phlegm making a vaguely familiar splat as it hit the moon.

"Great," Bob remarked. "Now you're spitting on the moon." Rob opened his mouth to retort, but changed his mind. He kicked at an antenna, wishing there was a pebble or a little dirt to raise on the shiny metal roof of the spacecraft.

"Listen Rob, whaddaya say we hike to that hill thing." Bob's fingers danced coaxingly on Rob's neck.

"I don't think so," said Rob. "We said we'd start testing today."

"But Control did tell us we had discretion in matters of priority. It was just a provisionary measure that we would test today. C'mon Rob, it'll be fun."

While the ship was slipping off into the distance, the brown patch that was their destination seemed to be no closer at all. Rob picked up the pace, determined to reach the spot as soon as possible. Bob lagged behind, beads of sweat dotting his brow.

"Hey Rob, Rob," he called after a while. "Rob, maybe uh, slowing down is an idea?"

"Look," Rob answered with an angry glance over his shoulder, "this was your fucking idea. I'm just trying to make sure we get there before Control figures that we died of old age, you know?"

"I'll tell you what then, Robert. Why don't you jog over there and take a snapshot, and I'll just wait over here, out of your way, for your all important self to return. Hey, how about that? Or better yet, I'll just take my imbecilic presence back to the ship and wait in the hold until you're ready to go home. Hey Rob, would that make you happy?"

They stood and stared at each other as the knee-high strands waved in the stillness.

"Bob, I didn't mean it like that. It's just, well, maybe we should – look I'm sorry alright? I'm fucking sorry."

Bob smiled.

"Tell you what Rob, why don't I tell you a story, a hiking story. I've got a good one." Rob rolled his eyes. With one arm thrown around Rob's neck, Bob began:

"There was this man who roamed about the desert. Sometimes, he would turn up in small towns wearing his filthy pair of jeans and a tattered long sleeve shirt with a huge frying pan and a plastic gallon container for water dangling from a rope which he hung over his back. He would walk into town, fill up his water container and splash his face, wetting his knotted beard. The children would gather across the street from him – he was a legend in those parts, you know – imagining that he was more beast than man. He had great globs of water sticking to his facial hair and streaks of dirt running down his chest. When he turned around after splashing himself, the little ones would take one quick glance at him and scamper off, anxiously playing the afternoon away until they could tell their parents at dinner that they had seen him, they had seen Desert Dan.

"Those dinners were always best. There were no arguments with Mom and Dad, no sibling rivalries busy developing into lifelong hatreds. It was quiet all over town.

" 'Ah, Desert Dan,' a grizzled father might say over mashed potatoes. 'I remember when I was young, I would see him, just the same as you, didn't look no different neither. Desert Dan, he don't get older ever.' And the children would pipe up, 'Don't get no older Pa? How come? How come?!' The father would help himself to another beer at this point, or scratch an armpit or bring forth one of his patented belch-turned-to-yawn noises. Finally, when the children were on the verge of another outburst and even Ma – with her endless patience – was preparing to tell the story her own way, he would go on:

'Did you notice, children, did ya happen to notice that frying pan the desert man had swinging on his back?'

'Sure we did, Pa,' all the kids would pipe in, almost in unison. 'Biggest pan we ever saw, and the dirtiest, too, sure was dirty, why, it looked like he never, ever washed it. Why it looked like... '

'Well, I'll tell ya kids,' he would continue, smiling. 'Dan used to wash that pot, he used to wash it every time he'd eaten, just like us. But one day,' and here Pa would pause again to suck in a breath, 'one day, in his wanderings, he saw a little boy crawling about the desert, lost and dying of thirst the way any little kid'll be if they wander out in the desert for long, and Desert Dan, who hadn't talked to a single human being since he went in the desert –'

'But that's another story,' Ma would interject, winking at Pa.

'Yes, well, Desert Dan went to that little boy and he picked him up and he gave him a swallow of water, even though he barely had enough to make it to the next waterin' hole himself. But the boy still was barely living. So then, he poured the rest of that water into his shirt and gave it to that boy to suck on and hold on to over his face. And then, Desert Dan, well, he picked up that boy and started heading to that waterin' hole which was, he reckoned, 'bout two days and nights from where they were.'

'Well, Dan and the boy struggled through the sand

and I'll tell ya, they was in the hottest part of the desert, the part where not even the cactuses grow, the part where the sand is like fire during the day and like ice in the night. Dan carried that boy through the sand. It got hotter and hotter and then night fell and it got colder and colder and Dan warmed the little boy up with his body and kept on movin'. Anyway, Dan was just about spent, he was so tired that it took everything he had to keep on crawlin' with that little kid just clinging to his neck. When Dan was on his last legs – and arms I'd suppose – he was still two or three hours from that waterin' hole. But he just couldn't make it. He slumped down in the desert with the boy on his back and just lay there, waiting to fry up like an egg. And do you know what happened then – can you imagine?'

'He was saved!' the children all cried out.

'That's right. Just as Desert Dan was about to go to sleep for good, a man raised his chin and dribbled a little cool water into his mouth and for Desert Dan, that was plenty. He got to his feet. A huge gnarled old wrinkled man stood in front of him. He was holding the poor little child in his arms. He said to Desert Dan he said, 'I will take the child now, back to his parents. You have done a beautiful thing, and for this, I offer you life.' He looked at Dan who just nodded. And then, the man took Desert Dan's frying pan and spat in it, a huge yellow glob of spit which sizzled into mist that drifted off into the sky until it was nothing. The man said, 'Eat from this pan, but never wash it, and you, Desert Dan, shall live forever.' The man took the kid and headed off, leaving Dan standing there holding his frying pan which contained the gift of eternal life.' "

Rob shook his head, escaping from his reverie, and noticed that they were drawing considerably closer to the brown hill.

"Almost there Bob," he said. They walked on in silence until Rob asked, grudgingly, "So Bob, do you…

I mean... do you think that –"

"That Desert Dan is still alive? You really want to know?" Bob smiled playfully. "Well... " he mused, staring out at their destination, "I'm not sure if we have the time... I suppose if you really want to know... "

"Bob."

"Okay, okay. But just the short version. Well, Desert Dan lived for an ageless, unnameable time, wandering around deserts, learning truths that only few, if any, ever really learn, and becoming a legend and a hero. And many a person claimed to have sighted Desert Dan and his frying pan so loaded with organic refuse and decay that it resembled the floor of our apartment. But, one day, some stranger wandered into town with a huge frying pan that they said they found out in the desert. Now, nobody believed that this was Dan's pan: this pan was scorched down to the metal, all blackened and silver, and besides Dan would never leave his frying pan. But a couple of weeks later, rumors began circulating that a little girl had seen Desert Dan take the slightest flame to the frying pan. It was said that as the grease and goo from an eternity of meals burned away Desert Dan's skin wrinkled up and aged until, like the contents of the pan, he was gone."

The brown patch turned out to be a brown patch. They stayed barely long enough to notice how their ship appeared as a small grey toy atop the huge plains of the moon. Rob scraped a bit of the brown surface into a small sterile box and Bob clipped off the top of the lone strand of foliage and trapped it in a similar sterile box as it floated gently down, caught up in its own personal draft. Maybe they felt the slight tremor, the imperceptible shiver of the moon's surface. Maybe not. Holding hands, each content with their day for reasons so different that it hardly even mattered, they headed back.

"Whatever happened to that black sweater you used to have?" Bob asked as he stared off into the sky.

"What?" Rob said, looking up from a small testing unit.

"That black sweater you used to wear, remember. Whatever happened to it?"

"Are you nuts Bob? Are you seriously fucked up? I'm getting this test kit together – you can see that, can't you see what I'm holding? And so I am, obviously, very busy, doing this, and you ask me about some sweater."

"Well," Bob remarked, frowning, "you looked good in it."

They performed the tests, taking air, plant life and small patches of the surface. Bob picked his nose and paced around the outside of the ship. Rob performed an analysis on one of the moon's growths. He stopped abruptly as Bob rounded the front of the ship.

"Here," Rob called out, his voice harsh and obvious in the silence, "take this and get me a deep sample of the surface." Bob stared at the tool Rob proffered, not moving.

"I dunno if we should do that," he said. "I mean, doesn't it feel to you that, well, that –"

"What, that what?"

"Well, that the moon is made of, it's well, it's somehow more fragile... more, more –"

"What?"

"It's alive."

"Look," Rob said, "we came all this way. We trained for years. We had millions of dollars spent to get us here, and you don't want to see what the hell it's made of?"

"Well, yeah, I just, well, I just think that –"

"Don't think Bob. We aren't leaving without those samples."

Rob held out the extractor, struggling to look like he didn't care if Bob took it or not.

Reaching out, Bob clasped the cool metal of the shovel-like tool and paced around the ship holding it at arm's length. Rob looked down, focused on the analysis.

Finishing his circuit, Bob walked in a straight line away from Rob. He pushed the instrument firmly into the warm surface and winced as the malleable ground shaped itself around the tool's sharp edges. Rob glanced up – his partner was just visible on the moon's expanse. Bob flipped the switch and held the handle tight as it began to vibrate. The surface, too, began to tremble, less than the machine at first, but then with greater intensity.

Rob made the last mental calculations. Dropping the kit, he realized that the ground was shaking like a horrified child. He ran toward Bob, screaming, "Stop, stop, Bob, turn it off. Bob, it's hair, it's fucking hair, stop Bob you were right, it's hair!"

The Moon shook with great ferocity and Rob stumbled and fell, eyes riveted on Bob as the tumultuous pink flesh rolled and then subsided, pulling Bob under the surface the way the waves reclaim the beach with the tide.

He loaded the last box onto the ship and paused at the ladder. He looked out over the endless, unvarying moonscape. "The Moon is a testicle," he whispered to the noiseless sky. Tears fell from his cheeks. Tiny hairs sprang from the salty wet pools he left behind.

Dad in the Dark Country

Dad came to the dark country where Dave lived. Dad wore a suit and tie. He came on business.

They went drinking.

The pub was sunk between two cloistered cobble-stone streets.

"This is an old pub," Dave told Dad. His favourite beer at the pub was something called #3. "You've got to try #3."

They drank pints of #3. A man came and put more logs on the fire. Shadows hid under their chairs.

"Hey Dad," Dave said, "Why do you think they call it #3?"

Dad told him why they call it #3.

"Cask conditioned ale," Dad said, draining another pint.

It was raining black drops. They started walking back to Dave's flat through the parks. One park was connected to the other park. One park was called the Meadows. The other park was called the Links. The way it was in the dark country was that during the day fog sat on top of everything so that feet and ankles disappeared. At night it rained and pushed the fog right into the ground.

The wind blew. Dad stopped and winced. He pressed his hand to his stomach.

"What's wrong," Dave yelled over the sound of rain through leaves.

"I have to go to the bathroom," Dad said.

"Me too," Dave said.

Dad stood there.

Dave unzipped.

"No," Dad said. Dad pulled the folds of his soaking trenchcoat around him. Streaks of rain ran down his glasses. He started walking across the slippery grass. He stopped again. He turned his face to the rain.

"I can't make it," he yelled.

The rain was very dark.

"What?" Dave said.

Quesadilla

There was this time in his childhood when they moved from one city to another. He developed this problem with his eye, during that time. It was a spasm, a tic, *a nervous unconscious gesture*, the doctor said.

Then they were in the car again.

"You aren't nervous," his father said.

"You have nothing to be nervous about," his mother said.

Now, he feels like vomiting. He wants to do that thing with the eye, but he can't remember how. The wind pushes through the windows. The dim light creeps into the apartment like a rat. There's a green pupil of mold staring out at him from last week's coffee mug.

"Relax," she tells him. She's on the phone at work. "What are you so uptight about?"

Once, he decided to make something elaborate for dinner. She was at work then too. After he made it, he called her.

"Made something Mexican for dinner," he told her, his voice shaky. He thought of his father, unblinking eyes in the rearview mirror.

"Good," she said. "That's great."

"But now I feel sick," he said.

All the Best for the Future

Raph moved up and down the empty hall. He stopped and stared at the notice on the bulletin board. The heart of the morning was beating.

"Sincerely, Bob Shantz," he said. "Director of Security."

His father hugged him.

"All the best for the future," Raph said.

"Sorry I'm late," his father said. "It's a long drive."

"Vacate the dormitory no later than," Raph said.

"Couldn't you do it up?" his father asked. Raph looked down at his duffel bag.

"C'mon," his father said, straddling the bag. "You get the zipper."

They stopped in one of those places that you drive through without stopping.

"There," Raph pointed.

A neon sign flashed in the window: Beef Bar.

The waitress brought menus.

It was morning and the beef bar was closed.

Raph stared guiltily at the stuffed owl perched over his father's head.

"Well I guess that's that," his father said.

Raph held the laminated sheet in his fists. His father slurped coffee. Raph got up to go to the bathroom. His father waved a menu.

Raph's father ordered. He told Raph he wanted more coffee.

"Where's the waitress?" he said. He looked around.

"I threw up," Raph said. A brown puddle at the bottom of a cup. "I feel awful."

"Big night?" his father said.

Raph pushed his empty plate over to the corner of the table.

"I've got something that'll fix you up."

They were fat and white.

"How bad do you feel?" Raph's father asked.

"Bad."

"Take three."

Raph hesitated. He swallowed three pills.

"If you have to get drunk," his father said, "drink fine wine or vodka." He cleared his throat. Raph cranked down the window.

The car lurched forward. Raph fell asleep holding on to the strap of his seat belt.

Do you remember the pictures of animals I had on my walls when I was little?

When your room was still yellow?

They scared me in the middle of the night. All the animals. Antelopes, elephants, panthers.

He thought they had pulled over. He thought that the highway's landscape was unchanged. He thought the exhausted sky was hanging over his face like a veil. Where are we? Everything else was moving. There was a great peace in the extremities of his limbs. He used his mouth to breathe.

"Fuck."

Raph opened his eyes. His father was waving the map in front of him. The car was weaving.

Raph drew his finger along the route, the college, the house, the creases between.

"You find it yet? Look for highway thirty-four. You got thirty-four?"

Raph's fingers drifted to the bottom, to the sides.

"C'mon already. It's coming up. Can I take thirty-four? Where the fuck is eighty-one?"

Raph fumbled at his seatbelt. His hands were trembling. He leaned forward and put his face between his knees.

"For god's sake! If you're gonna be sick do it in this." Raph's father handed Raph a plastic shopping bag. "You're not going to be sick."

The bag. His hand. His father's hand. A car. The road. Raph's body was wet.

"Eat this," his father said. "Your mother always buys the wrong ones. She never remembers the kind I like. She does it on purpose. She doesn't care."

Raph looked up. His father was holding an apple.

"Take it," he said. "It's not a mountaineering apple. They're the best in the world."

"Pull over," Raph said. "I can't breathe."

"Where are we?" Raph's father asked.

They got off the highway and pulled into a strip mall.

"How are you now?" Raph's father asked.

Raph got out of the car. He spread himself across the parking lot. He tried to take steady, even breaths. He panted.

"Do you want to go to the hospital?" his father asked. "Just take it easy," his father said. "You don't need to go to the hospital."

Raph's arms stretched out across the pavement. There was nothing underneath the pavement. Pull me up, he thought. His father disappeared into the strip mall.

"Get you some juice. A drink. Back in a minute. "

The earth would close. Raph's father returned with

a loaf of soft fresh Italian bread and a dried spicy sausage. Raph turned his head and saw blue running shoes, gray sweatpants lumping around white athletic socks.

"I found a fantastic Italian deli," his father said. "Right here in the middle of nowhere. And guess what. We're in Yonkers. Lost in Yonkers."

Raph got up.

His father brushed the dirt off the back of his t-shirt.

So did you have an unhappy childhood?

I worked very hard. My father died when I was still young. I had to do everything for myself.

Hey Dad? That thing about vodka and fine wine?

What about it?

You told me that in high-school.

"I always wanted you to be ready," he said. "That's all."

They took the ferry. They waited in a long line of cars. Everyone else was ugly. They felt good together, smart and good looking. They were assigned a space in the parking lot. Raph's father put his foot on the brake. He let go of the brake. He put his foot back on the brake. Raph made faces at the children in the station-wagon next to them. They got out of the car. Raph's father gathered up his bags of food.

"Snacks," he said.

They went up the stairs and stood together at the bow of the boat. Raph's father clapped him on the back.

"So what are you going to do with your life?" he asked. The boat beat down the crest of the waves and left straight lines in its wake. "Your mother got a new thing in the backyard." Raph's father was crying. "To feed the birds. It attracts a lot of different kinds of birds."

"Dad," Raph said.

"I'm sorry," he said. "It's the pills. They've got me on these pills."

Raph tore off a chunk of bread and ate it, cupping it in his hands, lowering his face.

"You're getting crumbs everywhere," his father said approvingly. The cold wind blew bread in his hair.

Do you remember the time that I came into the kitchen and you were yelling and Mom was yelling and when you finally noticed me you both burst out laughing and I started to cry?

Raph tore a small nugget out of the sausage with his teeth. He passed the sausage to his father.

"Good stuff," his father said. He bit off a chunk.

The Way Home

She looked like a hitchhiker. He rounded the long curve of the last part of his drive – hello! you are five minutes from home! straighten up and smile! She was running, tripping, acting out motion. He squinted. He was extraordinarily sensitive to weather. His wife said so. It must be the rain. He rubbed his temples. He glanced over his shoulder. He pulled into the slow lane. The clouds parted. The weather can never just decide. He put on his sunglasses. It was still raining. He was going slow. Trees and signs and other cars piled by. He stared at them. He took off his sunglasses. He followed the quiet strain of her body, the flapping of her feet on the shoulder, the give of loose stone and slick concrete. The distance between them. The colour of skin. She looked back. Keep going, he thought. It was almost rush hour.

He leaned over to the passenger door. His tie caught in the seatbelt. He wrenched his neck free. He stared stupidly at the open space of the door, a composite of stains and bruises, a dripping blue wound mining her hip. He got out of his car. He spread his jacket over her shoulders. This is it, he thought. He did not look. There was a way this was not happening.

She was in the back seat. He was in the front. The sun spread through the rain. The car was not moving. He looked at the trailing path of vehicles, hurried in the middle of the highway. The exact spot their lives collided. The way home. He remembered it from every other day.

"She just ran off?"

"I don't know."

"What was the matter with her."

"I don't know."

"She just ran off with your coat?"

"This headache." He looked at his wife. He put his hand on his forehead. "I don't know."

"Was it awful? It must have been awful."

"She stopped just before. Then she got in. I mean, I don't know, there was a second there when she might not have gotten in. I mean she could have just not gotten in. I didn't want her to get in. Get in, I said. Get in."

"You didn't want her to get in?"

"I don't know."

Between Two Old Ladies

There is a sudden smell here.

Inquiry Into the Receding Distance

An empty gourd leaned on its side. I buried his body in the field next to his hut. His flesh would not decompose. The dregs of spirit would drain from the length of his cavities but he would not decompose. I moved in. I counted the days.

I came here to marry Merelda. When I arrived she pretended not to know me though I saw her clearly three times in my sleep and she was beautiful and she was my wife. My mother held my ankles as I left so I would know the weight of the steps I was taking. The people here looked strangely at me. I stood in the square picking grains of sand out of the palm of my hand. The villagers gathered. Here, they said to each other, is a young strong man who has come from far away and is now dead to his family. Here, they told each other, is a philosopher who has come to our town to count the ways and calls of the possible numbers.

I became the philosopher's apprentice. I looked back into my dreams – even then I was preparing to become a philosopher. I stood in the square fingering the land's kernels. Words are numbers, as convincing, as perfect, as essential. I learned this from the old philosopher. I began to speak in numbers. I am writing this to tell you that I was never a philosopher, just a young man who yearned for the home he left and loudly calculated the distance.

Every day was an exception.

Merelda, I said. At least read the beginning.
She put down what she picked up.

This town was not even a town. I settled with them at the edge of the great forest. Certain words were not required: Visitor, traveller, adventurer, guest, migrant, pilgrim, wanderer. None of these things had numeric equivalents. I was none of these things. I told them they lived precariously on a ridge that overlooked a huge valley. Beyond the valley were the mountains. I explained that there were many towns. I come from one of the many towns, I said. Behind the town is the great forest. Inquiry is an empty box without compulsion. Compulsion less sincerity equals zero. And behind the great forest? they asked. I made notes. I crafted lists. I listened to the distance.

Merelda held out her pale arms and offered me the warmth of her skin.
I am a man Merelda, I said. Like any other.
Don't scratch, she advised.

Merelda dropped to her knees, touched her forehead to the crumbling moniker at the edge of the forest.
The land is change, I said.
I've never been to the mountains, she said.
I was above her. The trees were above me.

I am adding it up, I warned. I have invented an invention.
The villagers moved forward. I was older than they remembered. My hands trembled. I held up a crudely wrought screen. People gathered and argued.
It is a collector of bugs, Merelda said.
There are many kinds of collections, I said. That is the drawback of comfort.
Your hands are soft, Merelda said.

The road was dark and I had said too much. The juice spilled from his chin and the road pointed in all directions. He was drunk. He used his stick to talk. He said that it was me. I still believed what he taught me. He said too much. I inquired about the inquiry.

She was wrapped in a tight cloak. The sun came from behind us. I saw the scorched darkness of the mountains. I wanted to know when I could again expect a morning of such clarity. I wanted the knowledge of passing time I knew she had. She bared back inside me and grabbed my ankles. The mountains, I explained to the bemused villagers, can be seen rarely not because they are so small, but because they are so large. Merelda knew everything I did not. I looked at her face. She looked at the mountains. The sky shifted. She shook off her cloak.

The wind is stripping the flesh from the land, she said.
Nobody can see the wind, I said.

In the latest part a woman arrives for my semen. She raises her skirt. I am the one with the wisdom, she tells me. Merelda, I moan. The rug dries. A drought settles.

Years go by.
Merelda sleeps with many men. I write a long text that would have made sense to her. She refuses to read it.

The men came to me. I explained to them how to burn down their forests, how to see what was behind and all around them. I articulated the need for more. They understood. They went home and wanted their wives.

Desire arrives before epistemology. Logos plus

methodology plus desire. Rhetoric minus the accomplishment of hope. All this equals nothing. I came here to marry Merelda. The fields must extend into the forest. The land is crowded. The trees suck out what is fertile. I must do what is reason for me.

One tree at time, I said. In other lands where there is no forest.

I have never been to other lands, Merelda said.

Place and time exist in an enviable order. Flesh is the dream we keep having. She showed me the space. We saw it through the slits of our eyes. Merelda.

A gentle breeze pulled the soil around our boots. Hills formed at the boundaries. The rains never came. The soil became unhinged. The town was the only town past the mountains on the edge of the great forest. I won't go into detail. The town was not even a town. I held my palms still. I was dead to my family.

Merelda and the old man were wrapped in mesh screens. Tiny flies of a kind they had never seen before swarmed in their faces. The flies against the wind. The old man knew about layers. He knew about permeable soil. There were twelve layers of verdant earth. Then there was rock. Covered in mesh, there was no way to eat. The old man stopped eating.

I clawed at her mesh. She took my hand.

We danced and felt the width of the desert drag on our ankles.

Listen, I said. I came here to marry you and now we are married.

Loquacious

"What kind of blood is that?" She looked down at the stain, her lips already pursed.

"That's not the issue here," he said, exactly cutting through the bone.

"Well, what is the issue here?" She put her hands on herself, steady at the hip.

"Two pieces," he answered, raising his eyes to her chest, letting the knife fall where it would. "Two pieces of meat."

"You'll be sure it's done?"

He had to think about it.

"It's a question of politics."

The knife caught the glow of the gas burner.

When he sliced again, it was another question.

Full Hair Treatment

Stop here, Riley said.

German didn't stop.

Stop, Riley said.

German gripped the steering wheel. A plastic lizard dangled off the rearview mirror. Somebody honked, shifted.

Stop.

German brought the wheel around. Somebody swerved. The u-turn pulled them into a parking spot.

What's here? German said. He lowered his face into his arms over the steering wheel.

Riley opened his door. The old lizard made a bold circumference.

We were supposed to be out of the city by now. The traffic. The fucking traffic. German trailed Riley down the street. Riley followed some path, the sidewalk, the buildings, the breaking taste of Fall. He pulled his hat down tight. They were late. They were always late. He turned into the kind of building that makes up the edge of a city.

The lobby was lined with mirrors. The elevator was slow. German clenched his teeth. The fucking traffic. There was only one way out of town. Riley worked the elevator. He considered all buttons. His fingers drifted. The door slid open. German stared out into the lobby.

You don't even know where we are.

Riley stabbed a button.

The door at the end of the hall had a small sign on

it. Riley pushed it open. An empty waiting room, fashion magazines, brown wallpaper, a reception desk with no one behind it.

Riley moved to reception. German rolled his eyes. Riley picked up an unmarked bottle. He unscrewed the cap. He smelled the frothy liquid. German felt the backs of his teeth touch.

A dark woman in a white uniform took the bottle out of Riley's hand.

She looked at Riley.

This is it, he thought.

Riley took off his hat. The woman came around the reception desk. She guided Riley to a seat. A man brings everything to where he is going. A man goes through this much, and then has nothing left to go through.

Riley shut his eyes. He wanted to cover the seams of his eyelids with his fists. He wanted to keep it all, to let this be the single moment in his life when everything he was could be walled up inside of him, and nothing could get out. Arms closed across his chest. Eyes against cheeks. Pink scalp beneath blighted yellow hair. The receptionist stared.

Rush hour, German thought.

First appointment very free, the receptionist said.

Riley gazed at himself in the mirror. His scalp soaking. Red liquid dripping off the sides. The phone rang. Riley wiped his hands on a towel. It was German.

I've got the mold, Riley said.

The mold?

Yes.

You canceled the trip for the mold?

Yes.

That guy isn't even a doctor. I'm telling you.

Look at this, Riley said, staring at himself in the mirror. Just look at this.

I cancelled with Debbie, Riley. I cancelled with Debbie because this was supposed to be the weekend.

Debbie, Riley said. He held the hair in his fingers up to the light.

Riley clutched an empty beer bottle in both hands. Another, he said.

Debbie giggled. Riley's getting drunk.

German brought a beer from the fridge. Riley put his bottle down. One of his hands moved to his head. No don't it'll just – He scratched casually at his forehead. Under the hat territory was conquered. Shifting and climbing. Some discomfort, she said the first time he called. Burning, she admitted the second time. Very toxic, she suggested the third time. Using as directed?

German flipped through the CD's. What do we want? he asked.

Riley swallowed the rest of his beer. Let's do shots, he said. He could feel each finger's purchase on the empty bottle. German and Debbie stared.

Have another beer, German said.

It's so exciting, Debbie said. You must be so excited.

Something loud, Riley said.

Your annual Fall trip. Debbie touched Riley's arm. You must be so excited.

Next weekend, German said. He handed Riley another beer.

What about her? Riley asked.

Debbie got up. She pranced around to the music. The music was loud. Debbie made it louder. Riley heard the march of exploration. His hands drifted loose. The bottle dropped to the floor. Riley looked at his hands. No scratching, she advised the fourth time. Riley wrapped around another beer. He swallowed. He kept swallowing.

Debbie danced behind German. She put her hands over German's face. Riley could not get up. He was somewhere, anywhere – German and her in another world, the itching air around him where he was, her palms across German's face, his forehead, the impenetrable boundary where the forest gives way to mountains and hands join hands in excavation.

Riley staggered to the bathroom.

Cold water, she advised the fifth time.

The tap ran.

German turned to Debbie. His lips covered hers.

Riley's awake, Debbie said.

Show him, German said.

Okay, Debbie said. She put out her cigarette. She turned down the music.

Do it, German said.

Okay, Debbie said.

Riley tried to sit.

Are you ready? Debbie said. I'm going to recite the encyclopedia from A to F. But in Flemish. Okay ready? This is the encyclopedia in Flemish.

Debbie brought words up from the bottom of her throat. She murmured and hissed. She threw her hands around the apartment. She blew out words. Riley closed his eyes.

Full treatment costs three thousand dollars, Riley said. I took out a loan.

What? German said.

There are no guarantees.

We were supposed to be here hours ago.

It's dark, Riley said. He walked into the bushes.

Not that way. German grabbed his collar and pulled him back on to the road. The frost from their breath mixed and made a certain kind of silence.

It's cold, Riley said.

We better get moving.

German was smiling. Riley shivered. He felt his face.

His fingers crept up. The cold is numbing it, he thought. They strapped on their packs. Riley watched where his friend's feet fell.

I always forget about this hill, Riley said.

The air, German said. Taste the air.

Riley opened his mouth. Stuck his tongue out. The wind pulled at his hat and at everything that was under his hat. Riley hooked his hands under the straps of his pack. There was nothing under the hat. The air was the flavour of ice.

Look, German said. The big birch finally fell.

Riley squinted into the woods. White shapes settled.

See the way it landed? If it had gone the other way, we would have had to cut through it.

Riley saw a dead white splash on a glacier of gray.

Your eyes are better, he said. He hunched forward into the woods. I can't see it. He stuck out his neck. His lips were dry. He pinched them together. He mouthed a tune. He followed the bulge of his eyes with his body, low into the underbrush. His legs buckled. He went down. His pack twisted around and pinned his arms to his body. He hit the ground hard, still humming.

Fuck, German said. German's laugh. The cold wind on everything.

I'm trapped. Riley giggled.

German pulled Riley up. The leaves under them, cracking and crumbling. Wet sleet bounced.

Riley was blue. He clawed the seal off the bottle. He twisted his wet fingers around the cap. He brought the bottle to his mouth and closed his teeth down. He spit out the cap and drank. A light spluttered and caught.

Here, Riley said. In the sudden dim of the lamp, German looked bigger. He took the bottle. They stood in the cabin feeling the heat.

Shit, Riley said. What time is it?

It's almost ten, German said.

Shit, Riley said. He dug into his pack. Combs, towels, vials, gels. The pack deflated.

German watched. Riley brandished a large rubber cap with a plug sticking out of the top.

You can't plug that in, German said. He started stacking wood in the stove. There's no power.

Battery pack, Riley said, holding up a black box.

German lit the paper under the kindling. Riley held the bottle to his lips. He coughed. Ice melted off the lip of his hat. These trips used to be fun. Riley moved toward the stove.

This place'll be boiling in half-an-hour, German said. Riley held the bottle. I better get more wood and check the cover on the rest. You know how to turn it down? Don't let it get too hot. You remember how to turn it down?

It's freezing, Riley said.

But it heats up quickly. Remember?

Go, Riley said.

I should fill the tank too, German said. Keep the pipes from cracking.

Riley nodded. He felt the drops on his face shrinking. His skull shifted and fissured under his hat. Cold air. A door swinging shut on its hinges. He took another drink from the bottle. He pulled off his wet hat and then the bandanna over his head. His scalp clamoured for the treatment. He put a finger up there, located a wisp. He squeezed green jelly out of an anonymous tube. He rubbed the viscous cool into his head. He closed his eyes and spread the gel on every fibre, every loose strand, every empty patch. He thought of rubbing and stroking and breathing. He thought about bringing something dead back to life. Riley was concentrating. He concentrated the way the doctor had told him to, he was thinking about how he wanted his hair to be, how it should be. Riley wiped the sweat from his upper lip with the skin of his arm. The stove glowed red and heat reached out. He felt the haze of his slick head, the warm grip of plastic and electricity. Palliative heating unit, he thought. He pushed the dial to high. He was not how he was. He was how he was going to be. I'm not Riley. He got into his sleeping bag. He heard the crack of the fire, the buzz of electricity. He encouraged his head.

German leaned against the door of the cabin. He caught fat snow flakes in his hands. Red light ran through the chinks and cracks in the wood. It was late and his toes were fused together. He stood there. Winter had decided on something. The possible season of the air. Great snow flakes settling.

Riley, he yelled. Hey Riley. It's snowing.

German pushed open the door. His frozen hair ran a sudden shower down the back of his neck. He wiped his eyes. The lamp was out.

Hey, he called. The air in his lungs, a punching sore. Riley, he said.

He fell over his friend. He pulled at the sleeping bag. Riley's face appeared. German smelled piss. The stench of excretion. He shook Riley. Riley was still. German ripped the burning rubber cap off his head. Riley, he said. He touched his head. Sweat and petroleum jelly. Strands of hair. He dragged Riley out the door. He held him up to the unexpected snow.

A Great Adventure in the Capital

She had her finger hooked into him and she was holding on.

When he woke up, he was bleeding. He was alone. There was no one with him.

He rang the great bell.

"Bring sponges," he yelled. "And a rubber coat. We're going in."

She put the bucket down.

An Unpleasant Accident in the Lap Lane

The whistle's cord formed a layered enclosure. Timmy sat in the guard chair. It was him, his hand, his arm marking impatience with circular swaths as the old woman ignored the submerged directions pointed out by the black arrows.

Timmy knew what he wanted.

He wanted a reason.

Why nine-thirty?

There had to be a reason.

Otherwise, things would make no sense.

The old woman climbed down the rungs of the ladder, holding on to the slippery metal. Timmy covered his eyes with his hands. When he looked up she was busy ignoring the signs and arrows, the order that Timmy had constructed, dragging coiled plastic dividers across the pool's expanse, laying out the markers, segregating the future lap-swim into three perfectly plausible reasons: Fast. Medium. Slow.

The pool had been empty. Timmy had been planning to close up early. He imagined she knew he was planning to close up early; technically he wasn't allowed to close up early; but so what? Wasn't he in charge?

Timmy twirled his whistle. He leaned back in his chair and stared at the lighted shadow reflections the waves made on the ceiling. He closed his eyes. He opened his eyes and found the old woman. Nobody ever drowned, he thought, his mind swimming laps of mathematical analysis, the waves regularly referring to some irrevocable tide of sums.

The old woman swam. The whistle twirled. Events,

separated from their predecessors, became actions and rejoined the mutual pinpoint space by which the old woman could swim, the whistle could twirl. Only, who ventures into being, and who has being thrust upon them?

Take note. Pay the closest possible attention. In thirty minutes Timmy would have every right to close the pool. There are things that time will confer on him; so long as status and rules are upheld; insofar as order is not questioned. In thirty minutes Timmy could walk to the edge of the pool and tap his foot impatiently while the old woman paddled toward him. In thirty minutes.

Timmy climbed down the ladder. He went into the office. He emptied the garbage pail into the garbage bag lying limp behind it. He took the garbage back out to the other garbage pail which was exactly where it always was. He emptied the other pail into the bag. Dragging the bag with one hand he backed open the side door. He stepped out into the night. His skin as perforated as the air, free of humidity and chlorine, moved up his arm.

Garbage clattered on top of garbage. A glass container shattered. A can was crushed under the weight of landing trash. Timmy turned away from the dumpster. He went back to the door. He pulled the rusty handle. He pushed. It was locked. He reached into his pocket. He knew what he would find: Nothing. Every day for thirty-five minutes webbed feet propelled slow motion. There was only the curling and uncurling across a self-made tide. Underneath bright red cord white marks strangled struggling fingers.

Timmy walked down the stairs and circled around the parking lot. Dry rock hit the bottom of his feet. Bare soles crossed asphalt. Timmy leaned against the brick wall and steadied himself. He took a deep breath. He clambered up the short wall then jumped down onto the slippery night grass. He twisted his ankle. He fell. His head hit rock. The outdoor pool rippled black, reflecting empty stars. When he got up the past glittered, an aluminum constellation. He took a step forward. His ankle hurt. Underneath him was the broad smooth concrete tiling that surrounded the outdoor pool. Cool stones caressed his feet. He moved around the pool. He stopped in front of the glass. Moths bounced like lies against opaque light. Through the glass doors he could see the indoor pool. Across the expanse of water the office was visible, his keys in a tangle on the desk. Timmy leaned against the locked doors. The night promised a story that would never be told.

Mistaken

He went up there by bus. He had a bag with fish and more fish wrapped in newspaper – shrimp and cod and a big lobster still alive. He had gone to surprise someone he thought would be home. Instead, they weren't. He wanted to think something like: *This is where*. The stuff in the bag seemed to be moving. There was a smell. He banged on the door and she opened it. She didn't look hungry. He thought about the way she didn't. It seemed to him there had been a rustling before she opened, as if a darkness entered a darkness.

Big Stick Drool Boy

He approaches. She watches him as he shuffles across the sand, bobbing up and down. She sits up and slips a t-shirt over her bathing suit. Every day he climbs over the cliff at the far end of the beach and hunkers down in front of her. He drags a weathered stick behind him. He offers his hand.

Adeou.

Yeah, hi.

She wants him to go away. She wonders about him. He worries her and she hates his intrusions. Not now she thinks, not now. Not when she is so in between something that is not about him or anybody else. In front of her the hand wavers but does not disappear.

Adeou.

He is alone. He closes his fingers around her hand and holds on in victory, clutching to her as long as she lets him. Finally, she yanks her hand away in disgust. She does not understand how someone like him can be so desperate for human contact. And yet. There. She did it. She gave him something that she did not want to with all the bitterness and pity that act entailed. There. Her hand is her own again. The helpless creature stands at the top of her towel looking down.

Fuck off.

Adeou?

A line of drool forms beneath his lip. He tries to suck it in. His lips form a hole. He makes a convincing noise. He crouches at the foot of her towel, his stick protruding. She waits. He picks up her book and looks at it. His eyes peek over the top of the pages. He follows the twirling of her fingers in her hair. She stands and walks into the ocean. She looks out over the horizon, waiting for him to go away. She regrets the passage of time. It seems a waste.

He will go now. He always does.

She listens. She tugs at her hair.

When she turns back to the shore, Big Stick Drool Boy is walking along the beach toward the cliff, her money belt in his hand.

She runs out of the water, not thinking that it's faster to swim. She sees that he is almost at the far end. He moves languidly through the late afternoon, putting one shuffling tennis shoe step in front of the other. Her bare toes slap the firm part of the sand where the waves fall and pack the beach tight. Pebbles bite into her heels as she runs, her hair streams out behind her.

Come back here you fucker.

He looks down, hearing the curse, surprised, dolorous, ambivalent. He is approaching the first ledge. Tiny rocks peel off the firmament. They shower her as she climbs, muttering between breaths:

Fuck.

It's the way he climbs, not the speed of his movements. He knows every foothold, every problematic over-hanging ledge, every ankle-twisting crumble or thorny Mediterranean bush. Not that she is such a bad climber. Faster and stronger than him, and without the baggage: the stick and that made-in-Hong-Kong waist-belt packed with all the things that make travelling possible: passport, money, credit cards, traveller's cheques; things, jiggling incitingly in front of her. For an instant she thinks that it would take just as much courage to abandon them. But she hurries carelessly up toward the sun and sky and clouds. Caught in the sun, he is within reach. He is almost at the top.

She sees the cumbersome arc of his leg swinging

over the last ledge. She lunges as the scrawny limb moves over her. With one hand she holds on to the rock face while the other flashes through the air, cutting a determined swathe out of the day.

She feels it go out of her all at once: it is a loss of control, an imperceptible second made up of too-lates and should-have-beens.

She yells as they fall together, hitting the rocks below. He lands on top of her with a snap.

The water faded into the distance like evening coming. Her head propped up on a stone pillow, raised at just the right angle to appreciate the waning light.

Sight is one's companion through the world. Although, she thought, hearing the lap of the tide, it is not always accurate. If she had her journal she could write in clear, neat, black pen that sometimes things are farther away than they really are. And sometimes closer.

The prickly shadow of the thief was somewhere to the right of her head. But the amorphous lines of his insubstantial reflection were not after-images. It was him, disappearing into the darkness of the cliffs all around them. He had been there for hours, lacking the courage to approach her, his hand aimlessly digging through the impenetrable rocks with the slim twig he had found – a poor substitute for the big stick. She heard his slurp, the nervous sound of spit.

He squatted on the rocks, licking his wounds, looking at the thing he had found with his stick that day. He did not know whether to approach or retreat. The moment was forever, he refused to let it end. He watched as she flogged the slick rocks with her nails trying to find a purchase, a handhold... anything. The tide tickled her like a pet. She gave up trying to drag the paralyzed lower half of her body up the rocks to higher ground. He twitched as her strained giggles proclaimed the taut night.

He was closer, looming over her, less than an arm's length away. The water, too, insouciant in its friendly proximity. The waves cleansed the cuts and callouses of her feet. She did not notice. It was only when she felt the damp of her bathing suit against her stomach that she realized her lower body was submerged. It bothered her most to know that she could no longer share in the slow rising love of the ocean's curves.

She shivered from that feeling of betrayal. And not just that. There was the distance of Big Stick Drool Boy. It kept her separated. From what? she asked herself. From that thing. How could it be? But it was true. In the darkness he felt her fear and recognized it as his own: The secret buried under the beach; everyday he dragged his stick across the sifting sand, tracing imperceptible paths which were gone the next morning. He never found what he was looking for. It was always gone like the scattered lumps of delicious flesh that littered his walks, always gone until he finally found one which stayed or had he found something else? and they were the same thing.

Her. Self. When she left she wanted no part of him.

She is back in the past now and she clutches his hand with the disdain of love. A familiar grainy claw. He squats before her. Spitty warm air across her face.

Adeou.

Fuck off.

She draws him to her.

Now That I Have Become Important

This is the way I imagine it:
I make my way down the street.
The neighbours clap. Not your neighbours. Mine.
Can I help you?
The neighbours aren't clapping for me but for their dogs. By the time I am halfway up the street the dogs have all done their business. The neighbours have picked things up with plastic bags turned inside out.
I am lost.
I scratch my head. I try to swallow. The retard boy comes down the sidewalk. The retard boy! I love the retard boy.
Tonight we push the breeze through the streets. Tonight it is so dark I cannot put the key in the lock.

Mouth To Position

"Make a living doing that?" he asked.

I moved closer. I took hold of his sleeve. I made for his ear. I said:

"There is this place."

I was trying to tell him. I tried.

I moved my mouth into position. The way it felt against my tongue, drooping under the weight. I held onto his leather.

He played with the change in his pocket. He cleared his throat.

Amalgamate

On break this morning he is surprised to find everything wrapped in individual packages. For so long, things have been pressed together. Now this.

He stands next to the rest of them. He puts his hands over the stove. The water won't boil. The toast won't toast. He punches at the plastic.

Air Thick As Dinner

Perry opens the apartment door and hears the shower. Gently, he pulls the door closed. He creeps up the stairs. She puts conditioner on her hair, pulls it back. Perry gets closer. His boots shuffle on the hardwood floor. The sound of water hitting the bottom of the tub. Her breath in the steam.

They live near the factory where Debs's dad Billy worked for thirty-three years. The sky turns gold, then blue, then gray. In June, the air is cold, it breaks into hard pieces. Debs goes to work in slacks. A sweater. Then, suddenly, the clouds open. There is a layer between Debs and her skin. She pulls at her outfit.

"It's unnatural," Perry says.

Debs drinks beer from a bottle. She doesn't look at him.

The night is a mask.

Perry wants to go out. Just get out. When will the weather break? He wants to go to Suds. He isn't afraid: Fear would be something. But he isn't afraid. He suffers. He suffers from an upset stomach, from terrible dandruff, from premonitions of another unseasonal morning.

He goes into the spare room. There isn't much in the spare room. There's an old chair with hardwood armrests. The lamp sputters but stays on. It's a lucky lamp. The heavy base is a carved Buddha. Debs calls the spare room the baby room.

"I don't know why I did it," Perry says. He is on the

phone with his friend Steve. Steve does something for a living, but they never talk about it.

"She screamed?" Steve says.

"Yeah," Perry says. "She screamed."

Debs's father Billy drops by. The first thing he says is: "I don't know."

Debs stares at him, looking for signs.

He scratches at his head.

"You seen that sky?" he says. He kisses Debs on the top of the head. She nods. She's seen that sky. She holds up a beer, motions to the fridge. Billy has a red face, cracked and fissured all the way up to his thick head of white hair. He looks, Debs told Perry, like he once lost his temper and then never found it again. He's doing alright today, though. He's just dropping by to let them know that he's seen the sky. Tomorrow is his sixty-eighth birthday.

"Perry gone out?" Billy says. Debs shakes her head and points down the hall.

"Not talking today?" Billy says. Debs crosses her arms over her breasts. Billy smells the factory on everything.

"I'll have that beer," he tells Debs.

When he gets into the kitchen he doesn't want it. He opens the refrigerator and sticks his head in and breathes the way he does for the doctor.

"I'm going to Suds," Perry announces. "I'm sorry."

Debs gets up. Turns her back.

"I'll come too," Billy says. They look at Debs, at her back. The sky flickers incandescent. The factory dreams twenty-four hours long. Debs isn't sure how sure she is. Is it him? She faces the picture her father painted: A gash of fading purple, a dog casually rendered from an old snapshot, floating and exact on the corner of the gruesome cloud canvass. The door opens and closes.

Debs thinks. Arms straight across her chest. A frown with no expression.

Billy doesn't usually talk about the factory.

"Debs is more like me than her mother," Billy says.

"How's that?" Perry says.

"When I used to work at the factory –" Billy starts laughing. Perry claps him hard on the back. "Excuse me. When I used to come home in the morning after my shift I would see the most beautiful colours. I mean I would see incredible fucking colours, just there in front of me, and I would be too tired to do anything with them. And now, now when I'm not so tired, when the days are so long and my pension's in the mail every month, I don't see shit. I don't see them anymore. I don't see anything. Real colours, you know, they aren't so easy to see. I don't see those anymore."

Perry nods. Debs is like Billy. Perry doesn't understand either of them. The bartender puts a bowl of salted peanuts on the bar.

"Thanks," Billy says. He dips his hand into the bowl and tries to close his fingers into a trap. Perry looks away.

"You see the sky today?" the bartender asks.

"Hey," Perry says. "Hey. Tomorrow's your birthday."

Billy starts laughing. He spits peanut. Billy's laughing is like any physicality; it is a way to end things.

Perry picks up his mug. He feels the cold solidity.

"Will you marry me?" he says. Nobody hears him.

What is the family secret? At night, on the way back from Suds, the sky is so purple it is almost black. Perry doesn't know about stars, or constellations. He stands on the sidewalk across the street from their building. He looks up. She lives here, he thinks. Behind the squat building three smoke stacks point jagged exclamations marks. If the sky wasn't so thick, Perry would see things the way they actually were. He would see his bedroom window, and the silence of a lamp switched off. He would see spectacular colours.

Debs is in the shower getting cleaned up for Billy's birthday dinner. They are going to the fancy restaurant where Billy eats the ribs and Debs's old high-school sweetheart is the head waiter. Debs strokes herself with soap, lathering up her belly. She hums a song. The night is the old man's night. He worked the night shift. She remembers not remembering him; Billy as a darkness in the shadows of the sky, a temperature change, a night-light in the hallway distance.

And Perry? Perry is Perry, one way or the other. Perry is taking a shit and trying to think of something nice to say. He gets up and wipes. Mechanically, he examines the toilet paper, drops it in, flushes.

Debs screams.

"Oh shit," Perry says, "I forgot. I'm sorry. I forgot. Are you okay?" He pulls the shower curtain back and sticks his head in.

Debs is standing at the far end of the tub avoiding the water. Her skin is red. She looks at Perry as if just noticing him, his anxious face, his bristly hair beaded with sweaty drops. She laughs. That's it, Perry thinks. The end. What time's dinner? he wants to say, or Forgive me? or Shut up, shut up, just shut up. But Perry laughs too. The bathroom has a small window. A man in the adjacent building looks through with his binoculars. He stops, though, when the air gets too thick.

Perry shakes Billy's hand and feels the locked currents of tension in the old man's fingers. They can't both be like this, he thinks. Not tonight.

"Hi Debs," the head waiter says, grinning his nice teeth. Debs is wearing the black dress that makes her body longer. She stretches over to the head waiter and presses against him. Perry and Billy watch, waiting to see what, if anything, she will say.

"Hi there," Debs says. Perry coughs.

"How about the sky tonight," the head waiter says.

"Like one of Pop's paintings," Debs purrs.

"I hate fucking puppets," Billy says, looking around menacingly. "Don't come after me with any fucking puppets. Just keep them away from me." Billy takes a faltering step back.

"Easy there big guy," Perry says, grabbing his elbow.

"This way," the head waiter says, touching Debs with precision.

Perry is going to pay for dinner. He wants to pay for dinner. The first thing to do, he thinks, is to pull out my wallet and just pay. He feels the bulge in his pocket.

"How about a whiskey?" he says. "Who wants a Scotch?"

Debs looks at the blunt ends of her nails.

"Debs?" He touches her shoulder.

"Oh not for me." Her first words to him in two days.

Billy tries out different ways with his napkin. He looks at his lap.

"Nobody wants a whiskey," Perry says. He can feel the head waiter behind him. "Nobody wants a goddamned drink before dinner?"

The head waiter has a name. In this town, people are called Lloyd, Stu, Jack and Bert.

"Keep 'em away from me," Billy says. His napkin slides off his lap.

Perry sucks in air through pursed cigarette lips, he isn't smoking, he wants to be smoking. Debs puts the menu in front of her face. The restaurant gets dimmer. The lights turned low for supper time. Smirking, the head waiter puts a candle on the table. He leans over the glow of Debs's shoulder. He looks down. The air is thick as dinner. When Billy starts laughing, Perry gets up and smacks him on the back. Billy laughs louder. The head waiter shows up with a Scotch in his hand. Perry keeps slapping Billy.

"Don't," Debs gasps. "Don't do that." She is giggling uncontrollably.

Outside is eventual. Outside the most beautiful light escapes the purple-hued prism of the sky.

Her Moment of Eternity

His greatest fear was that an occurrence could neither happen nor not happen, so saddled was it by the brevity of subjectivity. He worried that until he did something, he would never do anything. He worried that by doing nothing, he had inadvertently done something. Why was he changing? He was aware of an acute awareness of the plurality of incidence; the moment was never isolated, but always illuminated and appropriately reflected. The imagination was a mutation of the possible, he reasoned, horrified by this obvious impermanence. He concluded that only things which happened twice could be real.

He was thirty-one.

He had most of the television shows and movies. In this he was assisted by his only friend Dave Valliere, who compiled a similar collection of images to antagonize his wife.

He did not masturbate. He watched the small screen. Lust is the envy of the soul. He put his hands on his thighs. He squeezed. Her hair fell across her lips. He put his hands on the small screen.

He woke up. He ran his fingers over his face to make sure.

The drama of the crime was the dream he was always having.

He dialed Dave's number and recounted most of the events in question.

"Did you do her?" Dave asked.

"No," he said, "I didn't."

"So what'd you do with her?"

"I killed her," he said. "I guess."

"Wow," Dave said, exhaling.

"Well I didn't really," he snapped. "I didn't really."

He looked down at his hands.

Snow

His job is driving.

He drives a car. He doesn't drive a truck or a delivery van. When he drives he looks out the window. He sees things, the outside drifting past, mirrored images reflecting back. This is my life, he thinks.

Only –

He pinches himself.

He keeps his eyes open.

Snow pulls the boughs of the firs down to the thin shoulder. Trees along a narrow empty road, mottled strangers dwarfed. Underneath this pavement there is earth. He thinks there must be. He thinks of his wife.

They cut her up, he says.

His hands grip the top of the steering wheel. On his way, North, daylight fading to gray, muted shadows.

He owns the car, he's owned it for ten years. He is handy with cars. How easy it is, he thinks, to tinker with a car, to keep it running.

He rounds a corner.

A woman waiting on the side of this long absent road. He hears the murmur; his small engine, his tires keeled against the loop of the tight wet curve. The woman is standing next to a station wagon. The lower half of the wagon is speckled with gray slush. He knows immediately. Car trouble. The hood of the car is closed. The woman watches him slow down. She doesn't wave her arms, doesn't point stupidly to her immobile vehicle. But he knows. She is tucked into an orange parka standing in the cold, arms folded and fat in the padded jacket. He can't see her face.

His tires crunch against the crust of snow, a miniature wall running along the edge of the winter road. He gets out of his car, pulls his gloves on. She looks at him, her eyes bright, full of the winter sun. His engine creaks, hot under the hood. The slow slumping noise as clumps of snow warmed by the late afternoon slide off the weighed limbs of trees. He doesn't think badly of her. It's nothing like that. A young woman driving North. For him, it's enough to catch the flash of her eyes. He knows the way the past looks, the retina imprint of pain, so recognizable, so individual. When their gaze meets, he thinks about her secrets.

He scratches nervously. The leather fingers of his gloves push his hair down in folds.

"It just died," she says. She shrugs.

"I'll take a look," he offers. "If you don't mind."

She shrugs again. "Would you?" She pulls in air, a breathless voice, the cold stealing into her chest.

"You must be freezing," he says. "Waiting out here like this. Would you like to warm up in –"

"No, no," she says. "I'm not." And then, as if seeing herself in the blinding snow mirror of his eyes: "I'm really not."

He can't remember the last time he heard his heart, his chest heaving, audible over the whisper of wind, time against his ears.

"If you don't mind," he says again.

He opens the door of the station wagon. He bends over and gropes in the shadows under the dash for the lever to pop the hood. He backs out of the car. He brushes off his knees where they touched the wet lip of the car. She's near him, standing over the hood, waiting. She has pushed the furry hood of her parka back so it sits on her shoulders. Her face is blank and expectant. The winter snow spreads around them. In the bushes, a rustle. A rabbit, he thinks, or a deer. He doesn't say. He isn't sure she heard. She must have. But the way she stands, rocking on the soles of her boots, her smooth forehead creased, her broad cheeks bunched together – her face falling out of itself, a frozen lake breaking up. He doesn't know her. He is disappointed. He can't pretend. In another time, in another place, she would have heard the sharp breaking behind the bush. And her eyes would have darted, their glaring curiosity like a jewel hung around the neck of the brief, bright winter afternoon. He's suddenly angry. He tries to recall rounding the corner, his foot easing down on the brake pedal, the peace of her standing beside the blue station wagon.

He pulls off his gloves. He hurries over to the front of the car. He feels in the gap, his fingers prying at the cold metal latch. She steps back, away from him and he pretends not to notice. The anticipation follows him, as if he was a boy watching the first flakes of a storm. The hood is open, he peers into it furrowing his eyes against the sun's slanted glare. Sunset, he thinks.

His fingers play over the engine.

It's the fan belt, he says.

Oh, she remarks. The cracked ice puzzle of her blonde hair shimmering in the welts of the sun.

You'll need a new one. He slips his gloves back on, each finger in its own confined cocoon. Another rustle through the empty trees. Or his own air pumped sweet through to the extremities of his body. This time she jumps, opens and closes her mouth, looks around. The road is silent, perfect, long.

A deer, he says. He smiles. A moose.

The blank fragments, her eyes falling to pieces. He doesn't want her to be afraid.

I'll be going in that way, he says quickly. It's no trouble. I've got a package to deliver in town. I'm meeting two fellows in the morning.

She stares at the spot; a snapping of branches; a startled rush of air against air; a sloping load of wet snow.

That would be kind, she says, pulling her hood back over her face.

It's no trouble, he says.

He hurries to the car. He opens the door.

It's no trouble, he says again over his shoulder.

He starts the engine. The urgency of speed, his foot cold in a boot pressed down to the thin floor.

The sun is abrupt in its departure. He stares up through the windshield, only half surprised at the voided gray seam of the horizon. There's a storm coming. He thinks of his wife, of the delivery in the trunk, of who will get it and when and why. She used to love storms.

The Centre

"Mother?" he said. "What are you doing?"

He was supposed to call her Mother.

"Mother?"

The sound of water was heavy. The distance between the tap and the pink peeling sink.

"Mother?"

He kept looking at the walls, to see if they were cracking. He was in his room. He was calling her Mother. He was supposed to call her Mother. He was sitting in his room. He couldn't move. He couldn't hear her above the weight of water dripping. He couldn't sleep. He dozed off. He woke up. He followed the damp patches. Small wet steps to the bathroom. She turned and smiled. The steam smacked him. There was blood on the mirror. There was a hole in her forehead down to the centre. She was smiling. She smiled.

"You should have seen what came out," she said. "Some hard stuff and some soft stuff."

Once More For the Museum

The net dropped from above. The mesh encircled him, hugging the convex edges of the toilet, tightening as he struggled.

All he had been doing was moving his bowels.

They recorded his caged motions, locking his desperation into their cameras.

They descended from their roof-top perch.

"It's a boy."

"It can't be."

"Let's get it out here."

Science was at stake. Why else the video?

I Do It Too

Howie is in his room. His face is serious. He is rubbing his mother's hand lotion onto his cock.

The door bursts open.

"Hey Howie," his brother yells.

Howie tries to cover himself with the duvet on his bed. The magazine Howie stole from his father slides out of his grip. He grabs for it. The cover rips. Howie's brother leaves.

Howie gets up and tries to lock the door. His hands keep slipping off the doorknob. Howie wipes his hands on the carpet. He locks the door. He stands in his room, naked.

Howie gets dressed. He goes downstairs. He sees his brother watching TV. He sneaks up behind his brother, thinking he will break his brother's neck.

The next day, Howie's brother helps Howie tape the magazine cover back together.

"Don't worry about it," Howie's brother says. "Dad does it too."

Her Dear Pitiful Kitchen

I'm skinny now. Are you satisfied?

I look the way I did when you first saw me hiding in the thick grace of trees next to the drive.

Keep looking for me. They keep looking for me.

I'm skinny now.

She took him out through the kitchen and into the hall and down the hall with its dripping shadows and old mud footprints. She pushed open the screen door and held out her hand. The rain was coming down, thumping the ground, slumping into the dirt.

"That'll be mud soon," she said. They held hands and watched the black earth soften. They were both barefoot. He edged his face away from the water but she stretched her toes into the spray.

"This is the way you listen to rain," she said.

He was a boy. It didn't occur to him to keep being a boy. The rain made him cold. They were not well off. He was skinny.

"You have to get as close as you possibly can," she said. She stepped off the porch still holding his hand. The point where their fingers met. A recession of history pulled back dry and empty like the skins of the cicadas they collected in the spring. It was summer.

"Yes," she said. "Let's listen to the rain." He shook his head. Everything echoed. He could hear the hard water crashing. He could see the tomato vines in the garden drowning. The space between space was slippery. He was holding on though, letting her drag him down until they were swimming under the thunder of the storm. She let go of his hand.

"Like this," she said. He was shivering. She pulled her sundress over her head. He was a boy. Her hair pressed down on her scalp in blonde swathes. The drops trailed down her body in mazes, crossing and turning and swirling, he tried to follow the progress of her skin. "C'mon," she said, her fists on his shirt. Everything was swollen. Was he naked yet? He had the first erection, one of many to come, memory saw them standing, tributes to possible tombs.

"Oh," she said. Her hands were everywhere. "Can you hear it?"

He covered his ears and ran.

They did this to me. And they did this to me.

They told me they would come and find me like she always did but that was just to get me to uncross my arms, just to get my shirt off.

Come and do it to me again.

He left in the summer. In his life it was always summer. There were no school days or short winter months that crept over windows with an opaque resolution. When his mother showed up like that, with a backpack and a bright smile, her breasts dangling loose out of a tank top, he wanted to cry so much.

"When is my mother coming back?"

"Your mother is crazy."

We hiked along miles of rocky beach. We came to a fat sandy shoal surrounded by cliffs.

"Let's stay here tonight," my mother said.

She taught me how to skip rocks. She waded in the clear water and I sat with my fingers in the sand. I was afraid of the water with its waves of imperceptible resurrection, I was already obsessed with being reborn. I didn't know if it was alright to be afraid. I wasn't sure how old I was. The night I slept in my mother's body next to the water was the saddest night. It was the only night I can remember. I did not keep waking up.

He is the dream they collect on odd mornings.

He is his mother's son, partly squandered in a white room with the shadows calling. Is she dead now? They don't tell me.

They had the most fantastic little existence, with friends calling and bringing jugs of red wine and big bellys of laughter, oh, they weren't well off, but the drive with the trees led to a cottage, two rooms, a kitchen, people stopping by, his mother turned over ridden like a golden calf.

Didn't I tell you my mother was a slut?

Mine did. She also told me about the end of the world. She put me on her knee.

"I think it's going to be summer," she said. "It will seem to happen slowly but it will be sudden – like a sunset, you know. After the first awful stillness there will be a road through your head echoing wind over leaves. When you know it's coming you'll open your mouth and scream with it. A smell. A smell like onions."

I put my hand on her nipple and stroked. In those days my mother wore a thin nightgown and drifted around the place, a ghost. She spread her legs, and I lost my balance. Then she looked at me in horror.

"You," she said.

It was cold in the forest. There was no one to make paths. He moved along the bank of the stream. No one believed there was a stream. His mother was afraid of the woods. She rarely left the cottage. In the afternoon when the humidity drove the clouds to the ground and the rain fell, she waded out into the tangled weeds in the front yard and closed her eyes. He watched as the fabric of her gown pressed against her body. The storm stopped as quickly as the clouds could turn white. The air was light and soft. She came inside shivering. He would go out the back door and slip into the woods. He didn't want to see her after the rain, he didn't want to see the way she wandered around the kitchen with an empty bowl pretending to make bread, moving her fingers, compressing the space of rising time.

He followed the banks to the stream, swelled into a current by the rain. The ground was soft and steaming. At a certain point, the wet earth slipped into the water and he had to swing around holding branches, his body a semi-circle over the clean rush – three feet of water he was afraid of. When he got to the curve where the wide tree had fallen across the water he talked into his fist, pretending he was an explorer about to undertake a dangerous crossing. Okay boys, he said to his fist, I'm about to undertake a dangerous crossing. He played alone. That slippery bridge. Everything was normal about the way he played except that he always got to the dark mossy instep of the forest just before the long shadows of the sun could scare him. There, he took his pants off and rubbed his soft body against the moss carpet.

Then everybody stopped coming. They were alone for what seemed like the longest time.

A white van stumbled over the deep ruts of that unused road. The van was very white. I pulled myself out of the thicket. Bits of bramble and bark stuck to my hair. I didn't know what it was like to have friends or drink soda from a can that tasted of phosphorus and refrigeration. When I passed gas, my mother would pat me on the head and say very seriously: "That's your anus blowing a kiss to god." I put my hand up as the van rolled to a stop and they got out, two men and a woman with pince-nez glasses and a brown sweater that looked like something dead. The woman stepped toward me and paused. The men stopped behind her. I could tell they were on their way past me. The woman motioned to the men impatiently. They shuffled on, disappointed. They were strange visitors; they had no wine, no guitars. The men wore coats and avoided the sunlight.

The woman pressed my head gingerly into her chest as if she thought she might break. She had no breasts. I ran away. Wait, she whispered grimly. That's when my mother screamed.

After there were certain amounts of hours spent visiting. My uncle took me in hand and showed me things I hadn't seen yet. Write that down. Oh it was all in their minds. Then I went looking for no tits with the pince-nez glasses. I was homicidal. I wanted to kill her. After he was sure to drool and wear pajamas that didn't fit and accept that every day was a month and that the days were passing by – ships on the coast of that part of the country where they came looking for my child-hood. No one ever suspected. There was a murder. He took to his room and waited. He wasn't going crazy. His stomach was sour from trying. He looked out the window. He stuck his fingers in his ass and thought of the empty dishes in her dear pitiful kitchen. He danced across the room, it was a small room. They took garbage away in blinding spasms of white lightning. And me? I wrote this down with long brown fingers.

God

So what's it like, living here? she asks.

Okay, you can say it. There's nothing here. This place is a hole. What am I doing here?

Well I didn't say it. You said it.

Sands turns away from her.

Let's have a beer on the porch, he says.

They take cold bottles from the refrigerator. Billy laughs as she settles into the wooden love seat. The field stretches, weeds swaying, evening breeze. Sands sits down, the wood groans, his arm light on her shoulder.

Sunset, he says, pointing a glass neck at the beveled gold sky.

Is this where you used to take the girls? Out here to watch the sunset?

The girls? Sands says. Ah, yes, he smiles, his brown freckles bunching against wan cheeks. The girls of God.

Actually, Billy likes it in God. When the long weekend is over she'll get back into her car and return to the city. In the city, she's an assistant to the director. In the city she spends the weekends with her boyfriend, James. How was it? James will ask. Relaxing, she'll say. Quiet.

Sands kisses her but she can't stop giggling, can't stop thinking: We're in God, I'm in God. She pulls her lips away, tastes inside her mouth, wet. It's Friday night and the town of God, six miles down the road over a hill and through a bend, seems like just another one of his jokes. She takes his hand, presses it against her.

Did they giggle and squirm like me? she says. Were they ticklish? Did they let you touch them? Here? Did they let you touch them here?

The way everything used to funny between them. Laughter muffled in silk sheets. Licking the tip as it curved toward her like a diviner's rod. Your dick, she joked, giving it a tug, following its point.

The sun set quickly, dark earth thrown over mahogany.

Do you want to see where they died?

Billy squints at the sky. Stars blush, blur.

He pulls her up. She trails behind him. A door swinging open. A sinking behind her stomach. Her hand in his like two links of chain. *He thinks this is funny.*

The air is a musty dress flung over her face. She pushes forward, trips over the first step down. Her body slumps into his, her arms locking around his spindly waist.

Jesus, she says, don't you have any lights down here?

They found them at night, Sands says. With the lights off.

Billy laughs, a diffuse chortle reverberating down the basement stairs into nothing.

Sands turns on the step. Halfway down. Holds her shaking body. His eyes in the dark.

I'm sorry, she says. It's just –

He leads her through the basement, its oblique possibility, its recurring darkness. They swerve around shrouded objects – ghostly luminescent lumps, furniture draped with sheets.

He stops and her body slumps against his, a flag wrapped around uncertain country. The giggle in her throat, she can't see, she swallows hard, traps mothball suffocation in her lungs.

Here, he says, in here. He pulls her forward. The sound of her bare feet slapping against cold concrete.

Another door opens in creaking protest.

Sands slips away. Billy feels for the wall, flails wildly. Her eyes lost in corners. Her body against herself. She breathes, tries to breath.

Sands, she gasps.

The light was on in this room, he says. That's how they knew where to look.

The blink of a naked bulb.

The sound of joints cracking.

This is where they found them. Right here. Kneeling like this. When they did it they were kneeling.

She stands on the threshold. Her palms press against the solid wood of the door jamb. The room eats light, its walls and ceiling painted a scarlet almost brown.

Jesus Sands, she says. Sands, Jesus Christ, get up.

Ah. He's crying now. I don't blame them. I don't blame them.

What if things had been different? What if she had been born and raised in the small town she's never seen, only imagined? Just barely a town, he tells her, two streets meeting, a general store, school, post office, church, cemetery.

Would we have known each other? she says.

We would have been friends, he says. Best friends.

Lovers?

I would have wanted you. But I would have been afraid to ruin our friendship. At least at first.

And I would have been impatient. Waiting for you to make your move.

Prom night –

You take off my shirt –

Your nipples in the moonlight –

I puke tequila.

Moonshine, he says. It would have been Daddy's special stock.

It's the same everywhere she thinks to tell him. My parents, yours, it could have been –

They sit in the kitchen. Bright lights, moths batting against the screen door. They hold hands, their elbows on the scarred wood table between them. Outside, the long grass restless in fallow impatience. Outside, something values the night, calculating invisible paths to impossible destinations.

You must get lonely, living out here, she says.

He shrugs. He's a painter, but he doesn't paint anymore. Just mixes blacks and whites and grays. Smells the colours, streaks them on his cheeks.

You think things are pretty weird, with me, being here.

Well they died here, she says. I mean, why would you want to?

Just suicide, he says. Nothing to be ashamed of. I don't believe all the rest. My Mother had cancer, my dad his heart condition. Arthritis. Nothing wrong with what they did. It was their time. They wanted to go, in peace, like old sick elephants lumbering off into the jungle.

She laughs, hears the sound outside her.

He kisses her knuckle. Leans over the table to her lips.

Sands – I –

She pulls away.

Ah God, he sighs. The girls of God.

He was once the kind of man who carried his needs with him, demanding things always – only – from himself. She remembers him drunk, swaying, slurring. He pushed her over, stuck it in. She looked at his blank face, eyes rolled back into his head. He's fucking himself, she thought. She slammed against him. Put her hand between her legs.

He was once that kind of man.

But people change. She knows that now. It isn't just something that's said. They change for the worse, they change, shuffling back and forth in their minds until their thoughts are well worn grooves and they slip into themselves, become more of the same, more of who they think they are.

Sands I – Jesus Sands. *You sleep in their bed?*

He shrugs, pulls the belt out of his jeans.

When she wakes up, he's not beside her. She imagines the note he might have left: Gone to God; or: Help yourself to anything in the fridge; or: I'm down in the basement. Didn't want to disturb you.

The bed is soft. It opens under the sudden shift of her body, sucks her back. She sighs, still tired, not wanting to get up, not wanting to have to know. It's the house, settling against itself, wind pushing old wood, wearing things down. She licks her lips, the dry taste of him, absence. Of course, she's the irrational one, not like him – just downstairs, making breakfast, in the back garden picking cherry tomatoes, searching through the henhouse for fresh eggs.

She feels the night table for her glasses, knocks them and her keys to the carpet. She flips over on her stomach. The bed moves with her, draws her in. She closes her eyes. But something jarrs her out of sleep. She gets an arm out of the covers, her fingers padding across the floor. Glasses, keys, hey, where's my – she pushes up past the blanket embrace. She puts her glasses on, examines the table through a sleep that sticks in her eyes like tears. It's gone. Her wallet. She slips out of bed. Her knees hard against the worn carpet.

Outside the air is hot, squalid, indifferent to the country it occupies. This isn't the city. It's supposed to be cool and sweet. She stands on the porch opening and closing her fists. She feels cheated by the emptiness around her: an amorphous depression of weeds, dust and blue sky.

Hello? she yells. She looks around for an echo. The clouds are faint outlines, suggestive changes in perspective. She looks up. The sun blinds her. Her bare feet shuffle against the smooth wood. From the porch she can see her car, slumped in the ground like a squashed beetle. The tires are cut, rubber ribbons spill out, empty guts. She half gasps through the beat of her heart. Then she starts laughing in mute spasms. A crow circles, lands, takes off again.

The basement in guttural moans, speaking its own language. She wanders through the darkness, an unlit presence. She hums to herself, a song she might have heard yesterday on the radio. In the city, she would be waking up now, the long golden arms of boyfriend James. Brunch at the local diner where the cook speaks a furious Greek and drops sweat on the griddle eggs. James pays, they part with pretend casualness. See you tonight! he says. She shrugs in the little room where they died; killed themselves; whatever, she says.

Her small dry palm around the string. A light bulb protruding out of the ocher ceiling. She pulls, feels the line give and twitch. Instant shadows. Hello? Behind her, the basement sighs, fades against its own permanence. She's on her knees. She's got her eyes closed. A hand runs down her chest, finds a nipple, pinches. The damp between her legs like sweat. *Sands?* She gets up. She slides open the shallow closet, finds the snapshots he took of himself. His face painted a gray blur, his eyes red in the instamatic flash. She selects, puts one in her pocket. She realizes, suddenly, that she will never see him again.

Six miles isn't that far she reasons. The sun sits fat

in the middle of the sky, a king on his throne. Or maybe I'll get a ride. But the thought of perching tense against the door of some burly citizen's pick-up – Where ya goin'? God? Me too, lived there all ma life...

Anyway, no cars go by. The minutes stretch into shadows. She starts walking. The sun bakes the fields. Nothing rises but weeds and fat flies. She keeps seeing cows in the distance, but when she reaches the spot she's fixed in her mind, the field is empty, the barn a burnt out shell, the livestock graze just past the next shimmering horizon...

She passes two houses that look like sheds, then a long white house that eats the ground bungalow style, a house hungry for land no one else can see the value of. God's doctor, she thinks. Or the mayor. Mayor of God. She's already passed the white washed sign: Welcome to God. Population: 336. So where are they? She'll have to get someone to tow her car, change the tires. Then she can drive back into the city, unlock the door to her apartment, lock the door to her apartment – the slide lock, the chain, the dead bolt. She'll cancel the credit cards. For now, she'll get Amex on the phone, let them talk to the garage, gas station, whoever, there must be someone. Of course James is out of the question. Visiting an old friend. Love that country air. Too bad you can't make it. Really too bad.

She passes the shell of a car, windows shattered, racing stripe faded to rust. Beside it is a green tractor, yellow cab, shiny black tires. Like new. Still no people. She steps slowly, avoiding the blister side of her left foot. A rooster crows. Giddy, she tries the sound herself, a cry captured blind in the timeless progression of late afternoon. She hears giggling. The sound is familiar, nervous like lingering.

Up ahead, on the edge of the yellow lawn. Two plump boys, arms and faces red from the sun. The children of God, she thinks, their eyes on her, impervious, judgmental. She doesn't laugh with them. She's sick of her own bad jokes. What if this is? – What if there really is? – Punishment. She waves to the kids. They retreat behind a plastic wading pool; brown mud water, sodden bits of hay, drowning insects. Their eyes are squinted, lost on their fleshy pink faces. She stops at the edge of the dead lawn.

Is this – she begins. They giggle and poke each other, squat grubby fingers buried in sibling fat. Sweat jogs down the back of her ear; the nape of her neck. I mean, she continues, where is –

She tastes salt on her upper lip, tries to smile. You two are brothers, right? They nod in unison, their jowels disappearing into their necks. Are your parents home? The boys look down, their expressions shifting from perplexed excitement to disappointment. One of them slowly works half a fist into his mouth, gnaws on it. Murky shapes swirl at the bottom of the kiddie pool. The hot air smells of dry grass and rot. She looks up and the fat kids are gone.

You from the Merton place? A woman stands on the house's paint peeled porch with her arms across her chest. Billy sees the kids, clutching the woman's legs like shackles. Should burn the place down, you ask me. We don't need that kind of trouble here.

Please, Billy says. Her voice cracks, her throat is dry. She feels desperate, more desperate then she is. Is it – is the town up ahead?

The woman shakes off her kids. She strides into the house, comes back a moment later with a can of ginger ale. She marches over to Billy, extends the soda.

Here, she says. Drink it.

Thanks, Billy says. The can is cold in her hand.

Shame, the woman says. Terrible shame what happened over there.

Billy lets out a short bark of laughter. The woman takes tiny steps back to the porch.

Town's just around the bend, she says.

Billy turns, forces her legs forward. Her walking shoes burn against her blisters. Walking shoes. She laughs in a steady current. Gravel pebbles crunch like cereal. She snorts, feels the air out of her nose in bursts. Two fat kids giggling. Two well placed slaps. Silence.

She sees the town as he described it. Three hundred and how many? She wonders if they changed the sign, after. Probably not. Two more, two less, what's the difference? She feels eyes on her like tight pants, revealing. She stops in front of the general store. Her hand grips the ginger ale can. Thin aluminum crumples.

The man inside the door is balding, portly, a little on the damp side. His jeans are new, the kind of earnest blue that gets laughed at in the city.

Just closing up, he says. What can I do for you?

She proffers the crushed can. He stares at it, mangled green against her smooth white palm.

Do you have a garbage? she says.

He plucks the can out of her hand, disappears behind the counter. When he returns, he's untying his apron. His shirt is also blue, not new, but the silver buttons shine in the slanted sun that trickles through the screen door.

Thanks, Billy says. Would you happen to have the time? The man appraises her, runs his eyes up. It's cool in the general store. Goose bumps on her bare legs, the work of some methodical pointillist.

Just past five, he says. I close at five.

That late, she murmurs.

He nods slowly, eyes fixed on a point just past her head.

Tell me this, she says. There a bar in this town?

Just closing up, he says, indicating the apron he holds in his hand like a shot rabbit. Was going over there myself. Name's Henry.

Henry smiles, showing tongue.

It doesn't surprise her that the bar is called Heaven. Or that half the town is packed into its suffocating press of sawdust, stale beer and farmer sweat. Five o'clock, hell, she thinks, Saturday night only comes around once a week.

She glances aimlessly around the bar, expecting and not expecting Sands to be sitting lonesome at a corner table, drinking her money and drowning Heaven's patrons in the expressionless swamp of his eyes. Henry comes back from the bar, two shot glasses balanced on each of his flat tray hands. She does a tequila. Another. Henry of the general store introduces her all around as Sue, his friend from the city. He winks at her as he says it. She puts her arms around him and buries her face in his shoulder. It isn't a slow song. He smells like the inside of a hardware store, lumber and grease and rubber. She met Sands in a hardware store, she dropped a package of picture hooks, he handed them to her. You putting up some pictures? The next day he showed up at her new apartment with a canvas framed in plain pale wood. She still has it: A small boy twisted in a ferris wheel rolling down a hill. Behind the hill buildings blur: house, store, school, church, cemetery; smeared colours: grays, blacks, browns.

Henry presses his body against new blue jeans. She giggles into his shoulder. When the song ends, she reaches into the pocket of her shorts and pulls out the snapshot. Have you seen this man?

A woman sitting at the bar makes the sign of the cross. Henry's heavy arm settles around her shoulder.

The Light

Paul peered down the stairs.

"Dad?"

He heard grunting.

"Dad?"

"Well go get him," his mother yelled.

Paul surveyed the gloom. He stepped down. His foot disappeared. He put his hand on the rough bannister. There were sounds. Noises. Grunting.

At the bottom of the stairs Paul heard muffled swearing. He squinted and saw a darkness in the darkness.

"Dad?" Paul said, feeling along the wall for the light switch.

"Mnt mnt mnt."

Paul closed his eyes. He flicked the light switch. He opened his eyes. Nothing happened. The shape teetered precariously and shined a flashlight in his face.

"Fucking hell, what's the matter with you? I told you not to turn on the light. I said: Don't turn on the light. Don't, I said. Do anything, but not the goddamn light. Are you trying to kill me?"

Paul blinked. The flashlight flickered. His father's flapping lips distended the darkness.

"What's going on down there?" his mother yelled.

"Is it off? Is it off now?" his father bellowed, sticking the flashlight between his teeth and reaching his fingers to the empty light fixture.

Hands to his ears, Paul nodded.

To the Sun

He met the famous woman under a tree.

Let's stay out of the sun, she suggested.

She said something about where she was from, something about her childhood.

He clenched his nails into his skin. He wasn't sure yet. It was real, wasn't it? He never thought she might have had a childhood. He took out his camera.

Don't, she said.

The flash lit up the lines of her face.

No, she said.

This Month's Promise

"How did the pain in your ear begin?"

"Like a pain in the ear."

The doctor made notations.

White watched through the glass.

"Did the pain begin slowly or was it there all at once?"

"It was... I'm not sure."

The doctor shifted. He fingered his tie. He wrote, 'all at once' on the chart. He read what he'd written.

White drummed his fingers on his desk.

The Doctor picked up his otoscope. He moved toward the patient.

White grabbed the phone on his desk.

"Excuse me," the Doctor said, moving toward the ringing. "Yes?"

Life After Wartime

I lived under metal slats. I ate red beets out of a can and licked the juice from my fingers. I slept through winter. When spring came I tried to picture myself. I knew the ribs of my nest, the nose of my burrow, the face of a cold chill. I felt the wind in my eyes. I could not see the city. Where was the city? Red juice coursed down my chin. It was night. It was always night.

That Kind of Girl

She took pictures of him and left. The lingering traces of white flash made his eyes bigger. The weakening of the chair seemed possible.

What if he pulled down his pants and then thought about things? Would his thoughts be different?

He touched his beard. The chair creaked. People don't know what he thinks.

He touched her on the couch. She pulled away because she was young and it was late and she was not that kind of girl.

This was not the same night it was so hot even the fan with the crooked blades had to be pressed into service. By then, clothes had become a joke between them. A spectacle is about itself. He wanted her the way he wanted everyone: Knees touching. The sound of shifting wood.

One Strange Country

On the way through they stopped at the gigantic falls. There was a darkness at the bottom of the falls, the meeting of all that coursing white and blue. He thought about god. Belief is made of strange places, quiet and loud, the rivers running fields down mountains, he knew all about belief. The mist caught in his beard. There are many ways to believe, he thought. The water disappeared in front of him.

He turned to tell her but she was not beside him. He looked around for a stick or a stone to throw in the falls, but it was all pavement and railings. They had argued at breakfast. She had become impatient and said that they were being mistreated, that the prices were too high, that the food would be greasy and bland, that they should not have stopped.

Enough, he had yelled, you are the woman who worries about the dress she will wear in her grave. She waved her arms about to attract the attention of the serving staff. They ignored her. Her manner was unbearable. He turned away. He pressed his eyes shut with the palms of his hands.

You, she said loudly, you will not say anything?

They were her people. All around, shifting and staring in their tight denim trousers. He did not understand them. He closed his eyes. He opened his eyes. Underneath his beard was his skin. She was crying. He touched the ruffle of her cheek.

You, she said, pulling away from him.

After, they had driven in silence. They had stopped at the great falls. The noise of the water falling, the silence. His back hurt from the cheap seat of the car they had rented. Everything here is cheap, he thought. Where is she?

He saw her, the bob of her hair, a muted red spot in the thick mist air. He watched the blur of her face. She was always crying. He went to her and told her that he was a shit, an asshole. She smiled. He put his arms around her and tickled her under her ribs. The thud of falling water, the smear of cosmetics.

Come, he said. Let's leave this.

Later, her lips were folded together. He would remember the falls. And when they were back in his country... He looked up at her hopefully. Her lips pressed. He did not like the land. The corn in planted, dying rows. Her hands were twisting a pretty scarf. He cleared his throat. He pressed down on the accelerator.

They drive slow, he said. In this place.

His back was sore.

They stopped along the road. He lay down gingerly in the dirt that separated the road from the fields of dying corn. A blur of brown and green edges rushed by him. Gently, she moved up and down his spine. Her balance was impeccable. There came from him cracks and groans and a long silence. She moved over him, one foot touching the other. A flock of black birds scattered. The corn creaked and rustled. She jumped up suddenly, bringing her heels into him. His back split perfectly. Pain flashed across his body. She was in the dirt, her skirt pulled up. He took in air through his nostrils.

In the car he stretched out across the rear seat. It was cramped. He slumped down, pressing his spine against the upholstery. When he closed his eyes, the crops rushed by him. Everything was divided. He opened his eyes. His toes stuck out from his feet. He moved them. They swayed together, and he smiled. His shoes were off. The car was really too small – not just for him, but for the country.

Is there any air blowing? he yelled. Are there vents you can open? He couldn't see her, but he felt a rush of breeze on his toes through his thin black socks. Relieved, he closed his eyes into the hurried dream he had of corn rows pulsing and rippling, conduits of frothing water, reluctant strangers.

They were late. No time to tell her about his dream. He opened his mouth to speak. She looked up through her mask of make-up. He was quiet then. They were late. He tied his black shoes.

Come, she said urgently. She scowled at him. Everyone in this country grins. All the time, he thought, living mirrors. He put his arms into his jacket. Now he was dressed. He was handsome. Then they hurried out of their room in the motel and down the small main street.

He could see the spire of the church. Her heels rang out, hard against the sidewalk.

We are almost there, he said. He stopped to smooth his beard. She kept going. She was farther ahead of him. He stuck his hands in his pockets. He walked slowly, holding his back.

She waited for him at the entrance to the church. There were many people with bow ties all the same colour. They waved, urgently pointing to the wooden doors of the chapel. He took her arm as the door swung open. Now we are the blessed couple. His fingers dug in, feeling the fleshy part of her arm under the sheaves of fabric. There was a space made for them. He wanted to close his eyes. He kept shifting. The seats in this country, even in the places of god, these people, it must be very difficult for them. He put his feet down flat on the floor and pressed his spine hard against the straight edges of the wooden pew. He winced. He leaned forward. She was still. The faces all around him. The music played. She took his hand. The music was too loud. Everything, he thought, is too loud. The bride was not unattractive. He regretted the bilious folds of white lace she was wrapped in. The priest was enthusiastic about love.

He closed his eyes and opened them. His hand was limp in her grasp. The priest was sure about love. Jesus, they sang. Christ. The preacher was the loudest singer, he showed his throat like an answer. Her recessed lips. The pews in tight rows. He closed his eyes and saw the stalks of corn passing him. When he opened his eyes, there was clapping and polite hurrahs. She was silent, now looking at him, now looking away. Her tongue, a point between her brittle smiling lips, a parted darkness. So she did, after all, belong in this country. He thought of the corn: stained fields frozen the colour of rot. There was a line to leave the chapel. They joined in when it was their turn. He took her arm again, and she winced.

Up close the preacher looked like a strange man. The reception held them in its fist. The room was hot. He did not take off his jacket. She had abandoned the cumbersome part of her outfit. The preacher was on her shoulders, on the straight lines of her arms. In this country, he thought, she is beautiful. He was holding a piece of cheese. He did not want it. He slipped outside the glass doors and stood on the deck. Inside, the preacher had the bulging eyes of his countrymen. A moth danced along the glass, attracted. The insects are so much bigger here, he thought.

He turned away from the doors. The wind lifted his tie over his shoulder and he pulled it down. Too many trees. He could see his breath. The cheese was clammy on the inside of his fist. He lifted his arm and rested it on the wood railing. He opened his hand. The waxen square spun as it fell. When is a crime forgiven? He looked up at the sky. The irregular constellations. The wind pushing against his beard. She will leave me here. He shivered, knocking his fist on the wood in front of him. He heard her laugh. The preacher bared his teeth. There was an echo: lines of running water.

Document

I asked him to pose for me. I asked him if there was a problem with this. He said he didn't know why. He said he was a happy guy. Normal, he said. He used the word normal. He asked me if I was going to want him to take off his shirt and wear the bathing cap. Yes, I said. He hesitated. He said he didn't think after all that this was a good idea. I said: What's a good idea? This, he said. This. This right now? I said. Only look at me through the camera, he said. You can only look at me with my shirt off through the camera. Alright, I said. He took off his shirt. Look at this through a filter, through the dark ribbed slats of your fingers, through half shut eyes, through ribboned lashes of monochrome flutter. He had round breasts and a lot of chest hair. He said thank you when he left. He looked relieved. Confused. He was fat.

Where did I meet this one? I'm not from here either, he says. I narrow my eyes. I motion for him to go over to where I want him to go. He doesn't go. I came here because of my girlfriend, he says. He doesn't have a girlfriend. He stands with the bathing cap in his hands. He has big hands. He waves them in circles. He says, I've never said this to a woman. I know, I say. You know? he says. I nod. He imagines who might come see this. No one will see this, I say. He counts the possibilities. The same people always see, I say, but there are also different people who might possibly see. He doesn't think about possibility. He only knows there are people who see, and people who never see. He holds up a black and grey textbook. Depression, it says in silver letters. I just stole this from Waterfords, he says. No props, I say.

She acted like she was once a real beauty. She jammed the bathing cap over her pointed forehead. She threw off her shirt. I watched her nipples harden slowly as if they were blooming young performers. I knew she would talk. They always talk. I snapped three hard pictures of her posing sideways. Her neck extended. She looked broken down. Failure, I wrote in my notebook. What are you writing? she said. Just an idea for a title, I said. Three days later she called me. How are they, she said. Very strong, I said. Strong? Powerful, I said. I let her in − I always let them in. I need the knock. The demanding presence of reassurance. She held them just so in front of her face. Work prints, I said, embarrassed. I look awful, she said. She was pleased. I don't even look real. Nobody looks real, I said. I snatched the prints back, I didn't like the way they looked just so in front of her heart-shaped face. She told me she was alone. She told me she was getting old. She told me no man had ever asked her to marry him. I would have said no, she said. She laughed. She told me she spent her mornings in front of the mirror. She told me she had nowhere to go. I eased off her shirt. Victim, I wrote.

He dragged the night in behind him. He was attached to the shadow of possibility. I adjusted the light to make his red red lips black. He seemed fond of himself. He kept trying to frown. Smile, I said, smile. Smile as if you are the only one who knows how to smile. I was kidding. After two hours we took a break. He was penitent. I don't know how to smile, he said. I want to know how to smile. He tried to smile. He kept talking. I knew what he was telling me was important. I wasn't listening. This is what he said: I was in love with the camp nurse. I was a lifeguard. We finish this way: He sucks his face between his knees and looks back into himself. In black and white his face under the bathing cap is a betrayal. He is the boy in all those pictures, the sweet boy treading softly on the future; a blond boy though he is not blond.

This is how we spend the rest of the end of our lives: Dizzy on the step ladder, looming over the wilting architecture of all of this. Was she the one who asked it? Or was it me? Am I your horror of death?

Would you like to touch my breasts? They are the ones with their shirts off. She takes a picture. Don't try and touch my breasts, she snaps. She breathes. She focuses.

Or else she goes to the movies. She wants a hero and a heroine. She can't watch when people die. She pushes her cheeks up against the folds under her eyes. When she opens her eyes to the dim theater, the light is a robber, stealing down from the projection booth. She studies faces, the gentle slope of theatrics, the place in the neck where things go after they are swallowed. She sits in the front row and laughs. The scars on her face are visible as a certain kind of pallor. There are footsteps up under her forehead. These are gigantic figures.

Camping

You thought I was fat until you saw me carry the canoe. I raised my fist and punctured the sunrise.

The faxes you had your health club send my office were not appreciated. I put the discount offers into big Phil's in-basket.

When I told you about it you said, You're mean.

You're the one who's mean. Phil eats and eats. You want to see fat? That's fat.

After I carried the canoe, everything changed. As soon as we got the tent up you slipped off your panties. All night I listened to the raccoons divvying up the garbage. I kept pulling out, saying, Did you hear that? What was that?

The sunrise was there on the rock on the edge of the lake. I held my pudgy fists to my eyes and watched the day blow up. You were still sleeping.

I Guess I'm Home

Mom, splendorous in a velour sweatsuit, gives me three hundred dollars in twenties. I think: A week's work, if I'm lucky. I think: I don't deserve it. I think: Why not, I'm lucky. I think: Are they rich, they're rich, aren't they?

I use the money to rent a car for the weekend and drive around with a girl I call Jimmy. She also calls me Jimmy. We go to the beach. The sun behind the tissue paper clouds.

"Do you love me Jimmy?"

"I love you Jimmy."

"Do you really love me Jimmy?"

"Oh just hold me Jimmy."

"You cold Jimmy?"

"Freezing, Jimmy."

"Come closer, Jimmy."

By the end of the weekend, our rental car smelled of wet clothes – towels, shorts, socks, flannel shirts – thick fabrics stuffed in a Foodland plastic bag and finally deposited in a metal garbage drum, girl Jimmy cringing at the wet slop of the sack hitting bottom, boy Jimmy leaning in to hear the swampy splat.

The way back: We pay the toll for the bridge. Toll woman sticks her face into the reclining automatic window of our complimentary upgrade and pulls it out just as quickly, her worker's button nose a wrinkled prune of resigned horror. *What's that smell?*

Girl Jimmy laughs. Boy Jimmy counts out what's left of his change.

Typeset in Meta
printed at Coach House Printing on bpNichol Lane
the text paper is 60 lb. Williamsburg.

The first 150 of this first edtion are bound in boards.

To order or read on line versions of this or other Coach House Books,
please visit http://www.chbooks.com

To be added to added to the emailing list, write
mail@chbooks.com

For more traditional interaction, contact Coach House Books at
401 Huron on bpNichol Lane, Toronto, ON   M5S 2G5
or call 1 800   367-6360